0/12

Prairie Schooner
Book Prize in Fiction

EDITOR
Kwame Dawes

Little Sinners

and other stories

Karen Brown

University of Nebraska Press | Lincoln and London

Acknowledgments for previously
published material appear on page
vii, which constitutes an extension
of the copyright page.

Publication of this volume was
made possible in part by the
generous support of the H. Lee
and Carol Gendler Charitable
Fund.

*Library of Congress
Cataloging-in-Publication Data*

Brown, Karen, 1960–
Little sinners, and other stories /
Karen Brown.
p. cm. — (Prairie Schooner Book
Prize in Fiction)
ISBN 978-0-8032-4342-2
(pbk. : alk. paper)
I. Title.
PS3602.R7213L58 2012
813'.6—dc23   2012001058

Set in Minion Pro by Bob Reitz.

Contents

Acknowledgments

I'd like to thank the many editors who have chosen this work for inclusion in their journals and magazines, among them Michael Koch, Jill Meyers, Andrew Scott and Victoria Barrett, Laura Mathews, Susan Firestone Hahn, Jill Alyn Rosser, John Holman, and Alison Weaver. Special thanks to Samantha Shea, and to Kristen Elias Rowley, for invaluable and much appreciated editorial assistance.

"Little Sinners" was published in *Epoch* in 2009.

"Swimming" was published in *Five Points* in 2009.

"Homing" was published as "Girl on a Couch" in *Freight Stories* in 2008.

"An Heiress Walks Into a Bar" was published in *New Ohio Review* in 2010.

"The Fountain" was published in *H.O.W. Journal* in 2009.

"Passing" was published in *Epoch* in 1991.

"Leaf House" was published in *TriQuarterly* in 2009.

"Mistresses" was published in *American Short Fiction* in 2008.

"Housewifery" was published as "At the Pond" in *Good Housekeeping* in 2010.

Little Sinners

and other stories

Little Sinners

We weren't bad girls. When we were little we played church, flattening soft bread into disks, singing the hymns from stolen paper missals: *Our Fathers chained in prisons dark, were still in heart and conscience free; how sweet would be their children's fate, if they like them, could die for Thee.* We set up carnivals and lemonade stands, and collected pennies for UNICEF on Halloween. We bought trees to be planted in our names in forests purged by fire. We drew elaborate peace signs on our notebooks, and watched the Vietnam War on television every night, scanning the faces of the soldiers for our babysitters' boyfriends. We included everyone in our neighborhood games, even our irritating younger siblings, even the girl, Sally Moore, who was clearly a boy, and the boy, Simon Schuster, who was clearly schizophrenic. They were cast as the frog in our production of *The Frog Prince*, or played the dead boy in our Haunted Woods. We would grow up to understand, perfectly, what was expected of us—and still, when it came to you, none of this applied. We were feral, unequivocally vicious, like girls raised by the mountain lions that occasionally slunk out of the wilderness of Massacoe State Forest, between the swing sets and the lawn furniture, into our tended backyards.

It was May when it all started, and the air was still sharp and the forsythia waved its long arms of bright flowers. My friend Valerie Empson and I had been stealing our parents' Pall Malls

1

and Vantages, hiding them in clever places in our bedrooms. I'd taken off one brass finial and slipped the cigarettes into my curtain rod. At prearranged times we'd retrieve them to smoke in the woods, and one day we put on clothes we found in my basement first: my mother's pleated plaid high school skirt (Drama Club, *The Tattler*, 1958), a cocktail dress (Wampanoag Country Club, 1971). We put on her old winter coats, camel hair and cashmere smelling of mothballs, her satin pumps, and black patent-leather slingbacks. We went out walking about in the woods behind my house, pretending we were someone else. We were too old for dress-up—this was our last fling. We put on the clothes and assumed other personalities with accents.

"Blimey, this is a steep path, I say."

"Where are we headed? Isn't that the clearing, darling?"

The woods were composed of young growth—birch, maple, and pine saplings, a thicket suitable for cottontails. A brook ran through it parallel to the houses, filled with brownish-looking foam that may have been the result of the DDT misted over us each summer. The planes would drone overhead while our parents sipped whiskey sours, and we lay on our backs in the front-yard grass like unsuspecting sacrifices.

"Oh lovely, I've gotten my shoe wet."

"Look at that, the hem of your skirt is muddy."

"Jesus, Mary, and Joseph."

We walked along the brook's bank, and I slid down the side in the high-heeled shoes and toppled into the water. The brook wasn't very deep, but it was fast-moving, its bottom a variety of stones, and I struggled to stand. Valerie watched from the bank, doubled over laughing with her hand between her legs. Pee streamed down onto the trampled Jack-in-the-pulpit, wetting her chiffon skirt, probably dribbling into her pumps. I felt the icy water soak into my coat. We were too busy laughing and peeing to notice anyone nearby. If it had been a boy we'd have been embarrassed. But it was only you, the weird neighbor girl, with your doughy cheeks, and your intelligent eyes. You looked at us laughing, and I sensed a sort of yearning in your face. That you were watching only made us laugh harder.

"You're going to catch something from that water," you said, matter-of-factly.

We'd met you years ago in elementary school. You were younger, consigned to the kindergarten playground. You carried a blue leather purse and were always alone. Drawn to your oddness, we broke the rules to sneak over to talk to you.

"What's in your purse?" Valerie said.

Your lips tightened with wariness. "None of your business." Your hair was cut short, in the pixie style my mother once foisted on my younger sister. You were thinner then, almost tiny, a dollish-looking girl. We laughed at nearly everything you said, most of it mimicked from a grown-up and strange coming from your mouth.

"Why can't you just be nice and show us?" I said.

You knew that you should be nice, and you did like the attention from us. Finally, one day you undid the snap of the purse and opened it up. We looked into its depths. There was a small change purse, the kind we made summers in craft class at Recreation when we were little—imitation leather, stitched together with plastic. Yours was blue to match your purse. You also had a handkerchief, a tiny pink one, and a bottle of Tinkerbell perfume. Valerie reached her hand in quickly and grabbed the change purse before you could snap the purse shut. Your face hardened like your mother's probably would when someone did something wrong at your house.

"Give it back," you said.

"I'm not taking it," Valerie said, dancing off a ways. "I'm just looking. I'll give it back in a minute." She opened it up and looked inside. You had quite a bit of change in the purse—silver, not all pennies. We glanced at each other. This would buy a few packs of gum, or the little round tin of candies we loved, La Vie Pastillines, in raspberry or lemon.

If you hadn't seen me fall into the brook, spring would have progressed into summer, and nothing of the business would have transpired. Maybe I'd have seen you riding your purple bike in lazy circles at the end of the street, but that shapeless figure of you wobbling on your Schwinn, those annoying plastic streamers spraying from each handlebar grip, wouldn't have prompted it. That you occasioned to show yourself, that this triggered my thinking of a way to involve you in some deviousness, was purely accidental. I'd climbed out of the brook and stood dripping on the bank.

"Go away," I said. "We're meeting someone and we don't want you around."

I took out the cigarette I'd hidden in my coat pocket and lit it up. Valerie did the same.

Your eyes widened. "Who are you meeting?" You took a careful step closer, pretending our smoking wasn't anything out of the ordinary.

Valerie put her hands on her hips. Her coat opened, revealing the shape of her new breasts beneath the dress's bodice. "A boy," she said. "Charlie."

We held the cigarettes out in the Vs of our fingers.

"Charlie who?" you asked me, suddenly wary. There wasn't a neighborhood boy named Charlie, and this meant that he must be a stranger, someone from beyond our subdivision.

"He lives on the farm there, over the hill."

Your eyes narrowed to where I pointed beyond Foot Hills Road, to the rise of a local dairy farmer's pasture. "How did he tell you to meet him?"

"In his letter," I said.

"What letter?"

"The one he left for us."

"Where did he leave a *letter*?" you asked, well aware that a letter was something mailed from one house to another with the proper postage. It could even be placed secretly in someone's mailbox. A note was passed between popular girls in the dull

4

hour of American History. And then I told you it was none of your business, that I'd heard your mother calling. You didn't give up, or suspect that we were lying. You wanted to believe what we told you was true.

I don't have to emphasize how often this happens, how typical of human behavior. The UFOs that circled our neighborhood one summer evening, flashes of silver and iridescent violet panning across the night sky, bringing us out of our houses to marvel—parents with drinks and cigarettes, children in cotton pajamas, all of us poised on our own wide sweep of perfect grass. The ghosts we've claimed to have seen in our lifetimes—nuns in barns, men with handlebar mustaches appearing in old medicine chest mirrors, the footsteps on the stairs, the "Light as a Feather" game, where girls levitate each other with only their pinky fingers, the mystery of blood and wine, the Holy Ghost we'd speak of when we crossed ourselves. You bought it all. You crept behind us and we pretended we didn't know. We put out our cigarettes on a rock, and we saw you bend down and retrieve the butts, like evidence, or talismans. You followed us up to the next road, and then to the dead end where a strip of old barbed wire separated our neighborhood from the farmer's field, where beyond the asphalt curb Queen Anne's lace bloomed and twirled its white head, and cows lowed and hoofed through muddy grass, around stones covered with lichen. There at the foot of the cedar post was one of these stones, and I pretended to lift it, to pocket something in my mother's heavy coat that I carried slung over my arm. You took it all in at a distance, your white face round with pleasure, while we pretended we didn't see you.

That night Valerie and I wrote the first letter. *Dear Francine*, I wrote. *Can I call you "Francie"? I heard your mother calling you in for supper. I saw you on your bike stop and turn to answer her.* Who can say what it is that makes us revel in deceit? I liken it to something pagan and impish. Weren't the fields and woods surrounding us a sort of pastoral landscape? There was the farmer

5

riding his tractor, the newly planted corn emerging to shake its tassels, all pleasant and bountiful, the smell of manure seeping through window screens into kitchens and bedrooms, awakening in us a sort of misplaced disgust.

And it was easy because I wanted it myself. I wanted there to be some mysterious boy who had been watching me, in love with me from a distance. I'd imagine that out beyond the bay window, on the street that winds higher up the hill than mine, a boy with sweet wispy hair and lips that are always half-smiling was watching. He saw me walk up the driveway to catch the school bus. He saw through the new spring growth of fox glove and pokeweed and fern, through those bright little shoots on the elms. From the Talcott View dairy's fallow fields, white-sprayed with bluets, I could almost hear his sigh and his gentle breathing. I could smell his sweat—coppery, the mineral smell of turned earth.

We left the note under the stone. We didn't actually see it happen, but two days later, after school, a hazy day warming up to be summer, we slipped back and there was a note to the boy from you. *Dear Charles*, it said. *You seem very nice.* It revealed aspects of your family life—your mother sleeping all afternoon on the couch, your father and his woodworking hobby. *He carves puns out of wood*, you wrote. *Shoe tree, water gun, bookworm. He is now making a train track that one day will run through the entire house, upstairs and down.* Valerie and I read the note in the upstairs bathroom at my house. This was the only room with a lock. We both sat on the closed toilet lid. The bathroom smelled of my father's Old Spice. This is where we sat together to read the *Playboys* and *Penthouses* he had hidden in the vanity drawer. Once, as little girls, we mixed up potions in paper Dixie cups on the counter—toothpaste, shaving cream, Bay Rum.

"They're all crazy," Valerie said. Her eyes feigned shock beneath her bangs.

"Tell her he loves her anyway," I said. "He doesn't care about her family. She's different. She's the one his heart is aching for."

My mother was downstairs on the phone, her voice lulling. It was a weekday, and my father was at the office. My sister was outside with her friends, watching the boys construct a go-cart out of a large sheet of plywood they'd stolen from the new subdivision. They were hammering on two sets of old training wheels. They would ride the thing down the hill, the girls watching, envious, waiting for a turn, and up-end it on the curb. This would result in Valerie's brother's broken arm, and a rush to the hospital in her father's Bonneville, her brother shrieking, his face white behind the passenger window. Her mother drove because her father had already started the cocktail hour. She had her lit cigarette, and she backed out of the driveway with a chirp, and took off with a squeal of tires. I remember watching them drive off, and then Valerie came home with me for supper, and she got to spend the night since it was a Friday, and her parents didn't return until long after bedtime.

We wrote the second note and said, *I think I love you.* We laughed until we cried at this, a Partridge Family lyric. Valerie said to write, *But what am I so afraid of?* But I wouldn't. Too much, I told her. We sprinkled my father's Bay Rum on the envelope. We'd used one of his old *Playboys* to write on, July 1969, Nancy McNeil topless on a blanket in the sand. And then we slipped out to the dead end. No one knew where we were headed. No one followed us. We had our cigarettes, and after we left the note we lifted the barbed wire and kept walking through the field's tall grass, its black-eyed Susans, dame's rocket, and chicory, the kinds of flowers we used to bring back in damp fists to our mothers on their birthdays. We sat down in the middle of the field, and no one could see us smoking.

"She'll look today," I said, predicting what would happen next.

Val practiced smoke rings. In a year she would be caught making out with Ritchie Merrill on the Schusters' bed while babysitting. The news would spread, and she would suddenly become popular in school, and we would no longer be friends. Neither of us could have known that this would happen. In our bliss we believed we were forever bound in our conspiracy against you. We would always press our foreheads together, and stare into each other's eyes, and know exactly what the other was thinking. It was the beginning of summer, and the possibility of days of endless letter writing, and grape-flavored ice cubes, and gum-wrapper chains, and a new attraction to plan—a circus in the backyard, where I would construct a trapeze and practice on it, flipping upside down, dreaming about being watched and applauded. We would have our stack of books from the library to read—*Flambards*, and *Flambards in Summer*. Boys our age would continue to keep clear of us. We would find evidence of them—murdered robins riddled with silver BBs, muddy trails in the woods littered with potato chip bags, and soft drink cans, and trampled violets—but they remained elusive that summer, and we were perfectly happy to invent a boy all our own.

We'd orchestrate moments to slip away to the dead end. Old Mrs. Waddams lived in the house at the end of the street, and once she came out and stood at the foot of her driveway with her hands on her hips. "What are you doing over there?" she called.

Val explained that we were working on a science project for school. "We're testing the rate of decay on varying thicknesses of paper," she said.

Mrs. Waddams pulled her cotton cardigan around her shoulders. You could almost smell the mothballs, the lilac powder she fluffed between her breasts. Her hands were gnarled like the branches of her crabapple. She made a noise as if she didn't believe us, and turned away and shuffled into her house. As a teenager, after we'd moved away from the neighborhood, I would bring boys to the dead end to have sex, and sometimes we'd fall asleep in the car. The next morning old Mrs. Waddams, still vigilant, would come to the fogged-over car window and rap her bony fist. "You in there," she'd say. "Are you alive? Wake up!" She would see us scramble to rearrange our clothes, embarrassed by our bodies, as if what we had done with them had nothing to do with the pale skin showing in the morning light, the sex a ritual, and empty after, like the one thing we had hoped for had died, and we were dead along with it.

The farmer boy didn't need to write much in his letters to convince you. We created his messy cursive. He said he had chores on the farm, and he hunted and fished in the little pond we'd seen when we went on our explorations as children, choosing a swath of a green hillside showing over the trees in the distance, and heading out with Scout canteens and peanut butter crackers. You had plenty to write about, your letters growing longer, written in colored ink on lined notebook paper. You drew designs along the borders—swirling paisley, hearts and moons and stars and clusters of grapes. You filled the pages with clever stories about your family and your pet gerbils, Hansel and Gretel. *Today we had an adventure!* you'd written. *Gretel escaped and is currently unaccounted for. The King and Queen are beside themselves thinking they will put a foot into a shoe where she is hiding and crush her.* And *Oh, the plight of a lost gerbil is one we will never have to endure. So small! And the world so large!*

It didn't matter what we wrote back. Any sort of acknowledgment seemed enough to keep you writing. When you were punished for some small household infraction: *My bedroom is a tower, and I will forever watch the world from it.* And *I am thrown into the dungeon and the blackness is deep and desolate. Then I remember you, writing from your sunny field, waiting in the woods to retrieve my letter. You are Lancelot, Tirra lira.* Your letters cast a pall over that summer. We came to know all of your flourishes and games, your mundane details: what color you painted your nails (*skinny dip*), how much money you'd saved watering the vacationing neighbor's philodendron, and what you intended to do with it (*buy a ticket to France to meet my pen pal Chantal*). We learned of your disappointment in never knowing where the balloon you released in science class ended up (*Oh, where oh* where? Zimbabwe? Tahiti? Scranton?). You described your week-long beach vacation (*seaside manse*), your father in his swimsuit (*hairy thighs, and the conspicuous lump, like something alive stuffed in his skimpy trunks*).

We never knew exactly what to make of your revelations. They became things Val and I thought we should not know, like the questions and answers in the *Penthouse* forum. *The King is on a rampage this morning. The Queen has spent too much money on summer clothes and groceries and other means of existence. Meanwhile the King is busy with his hobbies, and refuses to seek another position in the kingdom. Tonight we dine on canned Beeferoni. The Queen puts it on the Royal Doulton.* "Don't be a cunt," the King says, in the foulest of humors. Charlie, the farmer boy, was boring, his domain limited. We couldn't imagine anything else to fill his life. Faced with your letters, growing longer and more intimate, his became brief, like jotted-down lists. *Work to do today*, he'd write. *Build the fence down by the road. Caught some nice perch this morning.* His only allure was his mysteriousness.

Finally, it seemed you were tapped. It was late July, a heat wave. We hunkered down in my basement and played naked Barbies. *Show yourself to me*, you wrote. Years later I would have a letter-writing affair with a man. It was thrilling at first, to see his slanted script, to learn who he was, or who he wanted me to believe he was. I imagine, with writing, the words on the page unfurling like little banners, their meanings cryptic, that we can never know what anyone intended. I put off meeting him, despite his numerous attempts and arrangements. I could never be sure, in the end, if the feelings he revealed were authentic, or just a guise to lure me into having sex. He tired of just the writing, and getting nothing, and that summer we grew tired of it as well.

We became careless and silly. We asked you to leave a pair of your underwear under the stone. *If you do*, Charlie wrote, *I'll meet you.* It was so ridiculous we didn't believe you would do it.

We thought that would be the end of it, that you would know the truth. I remember the day Val went up to the dead end to check. We'd begun doing it separately, to avoid detection. She'd come to my door and my mother let her in.

"*Vite! Vite!*" she cried, tugging on my arm. Her breath smelled of cigarettes.

My mother was in the middle of something—folding laundry, or making lunch, or swiping the tables with Pledge. She never knew. Parents don't, even when they think they do. I expected Val to pull the underwear out of her pocket, but she said, no, she wouldn't touch it. So the two of us headed up the street. Of course, we were spotted by some of the younger neighborhood kids who'd been suspicious of us from the beginning. It was a small gang of us watching as Val lifted the underwear up in the air with a stick, holding it there like a flag. It was a simple pair, pale and slightly grayed from washing, a small flower attached to the elastic waistband. Soon, for all of us, there would be that splash of bright blood, and we knew it then, and it terrified us. I imagined my own underwear, tucked in the darkness of my top bureau drawer, exposed against the contrast of sunlight and waving grass, the starkness of the stone, the asphalt, the barbed wire tines, the decaying cedar post.

We were done with the letter writing, with the whole game. We didn't care what happened next, or who knew. I can't remember if we told everyone, or if the boy who grabbed the stick and the underwear and raced off on his bike knew who they belonged to. I didn't think it mattered. I see the group of us parading back down our street, the boy at the lead, looking like the benign children depicted in Joan Walsh Anglund prints, with their chunky limbs, large foreheads, heavy bangs, eyes like dark pinpricks.

That night we stayed out late, organizing yard games for the neighborhood kids: Freeze Tag, Red Rover, Mother-May-I, What Time Is It? We played until we could no longer see each other in the darkness, until the fireflies began their heated blinking, bobbing and elusive along the edge of the woods, until the mothers, standing in clusters with their cigarettes and drinks, called everyone in. We went to bed with grass-stained feet, our hair smelling like sun and sweat. And the next morning you were gone. The phone rang and the news came from the Schusters. The police parked in front of your house. Val and I stood with everyone at the end of your driveway, waiting for word. Your mother was there, roused from her couch, her eyes red-rimmed, her hands large and veined and clutching something we learned was the baby blanket you still slept with. Your father was there, an older-looking man, hunched over in a sports shirt.

"Geppetto," Val whispered. We both laughed, nervous laughter you might have forgiven us for.

Your bike was found at the dead end. And it wouldn't take long for some of the story to come out, but just part of it about a boy writing you notes. No one knew who the boy was, or where he lived, and all of the neighborhood boys were questioned, the police going house to house. Val and I said it was like "Cinderella," when the prince goes through the village trying to ferret out the young woman whose foot fit the slipper. We stuck together all that day, waiting for the letters we'd written to be discovered, but they were not. We imagined you'd hidden them in some old book, Lord Alfred Tennyson's *Poems*, the pages carved out beneath the mildewed cover. We thought we knew you then, as well as we knew ourselves. Still, we said nothing, our hearts soft and quick like the robins we'd find near death. Search parties were organized—neighborhood people, volunteer firemen from the town over. Mothers made sandwiches. The men combed the woods along the little brook, climbed over barbed wire and waded into the maze of cornfields. *Francie! Francie!* The sound of your name became a refrain. Long into the evening hours we listened to the way it went, back and forth, from all sides surrounding our neighborhood, echoing back off the rows of houses, the shake shingles and the aluminum siding.

There was a fear of abduction. There'd been little Janice Pockett on the news the summer before, who'd gone out on her bike to retrieve a butterfly and never returned. We'd seen the photos of her on flyers—blond hair and freckles and blue eyes, slightly crooked teeth—the newspaper articles documenting the search, and the giving up on searching, until she became just someone missing, a girl whose mother continued to "hold out hope." I am still plagued by that girl's eyes staring out from some third-grade school portrait, the way life shines in them, alert and potent, waiting to be lived. Val and I stayed together, consigned to our yards. The general fear of the unknown took over, and we gathered in hushed groups to imagine what might have happened to you. No one mentioned the underwear, tossed over the fence into the pasture, trampled into the grass by the farmer's cows. But they were found by the searchers, and cataloged as grim evidence. Val was called home earlier than usual, and we separated, worrying what the other might, in a moment of weakness, confess. At night every deadbolt turned. I lay in bed listening to the crickets, the frogs in the brook, the pinging of beetles against the metal window screen, sounds that I can still imagine, that make me think of the child I was, and the woman I am now, and how little I understood of my life, and how little I still understand.

You weren't taken away by a stranger. A maroon car didn't pull over and scoop you into its dank upholstered depths. Near morning they found you nestled at the base of a pine tree a mile away. You suffered from mosquito bites and dehydration. They brought you back wrapped in a pink blanket, your hair disheveled and stuck with pine needles. We watched from the safety of someone else's front lawn. The police were there, and the fireman who found you, and your parents. Your mother swooned onto the dewy grass and the fireman caught her. Your father stood apart, shaking his head, his hands on his hips, as if to chastise the two of you. I imagined wood shavings were caught in his gray curls. I remembered the word he called your mother. No one could fathom your resolve to stay hidden, to avoid the comfort of your own bed, the stuffed animals and porcelain figurines that lined your bedroom shelves, staring down at you with their frozen, wise looks. I watched you brought home and I felt, even then, the widening rift between myself and that world of mown grass and tree canopies, the race of years, their rush to overwhelm me.

You never told. But I remember the story you wrote to the boy you may have known all along was pretend. Someone came into your room, you'd written. *His breath smelled of crème de menthe. His hands were furry, like a wild beast's.* You told the searchers that you'd fallen asleep in the woods. You didn't expect them to believe you, but they could come up with no other alternative. We never checked under the stone again, but one night with a boy at the dead end I lifted it one last time and sifted through the dirt. I imagined I saw the decaying pieces of what may have been your last installment. In all stories are the seeds of what we cannot say out loud—that we are corporeal, left to the mercy of the body's urges. You never married. Your mother died of breast cancer, and you fought for years, seeking to lay blame on our corrupted well water, citing the incidences of cancer in our neighbors. My sister sent me the article you wrote, and your picture—a taller version of you than I remembered, standing in the doorway of your mother's split-level. I imagined your father doddering about in the dim interior. You have one arm held across your chest like a shield, stalwart with your secret. Nothing ever came of your fury, your petitions. Today I discovered that you succumbed, too, of the same disease as your mother.

That night you disappeared, I'd lain in bed and imagined you in the arms of a boy I'd invented, his hair a shock of blond over his eyes, from his mouth a hum like the drone of hornets nesting in the garage. I see your face, rounded with joy, the way it looked retrieving the letter from under the stone. This is the way I like to recall it. The neighborhood remains, the farm and the farmer's fields. In summer the corn does its fine green swaying dance.

In thunderstorms the lightning arcs and cleaves and the air fills with ozone. The houses still line the street in their same order. How much stays the same is undeniable, but I am unsure how much this reassures anyone. I no longer go back. What would be the point of revisiting it? We are all alone with the stories we have never told, and even now, given your death, there is no real forgiveness. Just this acknowledgment, whatever it is worth, of all the little deaths that came before it.

Swimming

Memorial Day in Sunset Bayou begins and ends with drinks in an organized circuit of the neighborhood. The following morning everyone awakens to some form of destruction. The St. Augustine flattened and muddied, blown debris caught in the Winslows' gardenia hedge, left under the Barringtons' cast-iron recliners—lipstick-stained napkins, toothpick American flags, shards of Noritake, a pair of beaded mules with a broken heel. They'd face highball glasses abandoned on patio bars, the deteriorated lime floating in the remains of gin, pools littered with grass and empty cigarette packs and a Monarch or two, struggling weakly, tragically, on the surface of the chlorinated water.

Elise felt the pull of repetition, the ease with which she was drawn, like everyone, as if into the spokes of a wheel. The day had a history for them. It furnished nostalgia and a dry taste on the tongue like vermouth. She kept the memories of the day bundled together, everything tinged with the remorse of hangover. Her husband, Will, grew giddy at its approach. The yardmen were summoned early. Will joined them outside trimming back the ancient philodendron, his body wiry, wielding the machete. The men went about their work with their headphones and their powerful mowers, ignoring him, irritated by his zealousness.

This year would be their twelfth in the neighborhood. There was one new house added, a young couple from Rhode Island who had purchased their two-story Colonial in March. The wife was a tall blond named Simone. Already Elise had overheard Will and a few neighborhood men, standing at the end of their driveway one evening with cigars, tag her "the Masseuse." Her husband's name was Doug. He was equally tall and well built and put the other husbands to shame by letting the neighborhood children abuse his lawn with games of baseball, and so was treated with an off-handed friendliness that didn't quite mask disregard. They would take the place of Gil and Josie Miller (appetizers/lunch), who had succumbed to divorce. Elise wondered what they would make of the day, what seeds of regret they would take, miserably drunk, to bed with them that evening.

But at the start of the Memorial Day rounds, Simone and Doug politely refused the mimosas at breakfast.

"Something else?" Gina Beldon asked, her little hands poised in the air like two wings, her eyes round. "Bloody Mary?" she suggested. Everyone mingled on the dewy lawn, lined up with plates at silver chafing dishes holding eggs Benedict. It was nine o'clock. Simone smiled at her, showing brilliant teeth.

"Orange juice is fine," she said. "Your magnolia smells wonderful."

The tree bore large, saucer-shaped blooms. Those who'd overheard looked around and up, searching out the scent that had not occurred to them. Eventually, no one noticed that Doug and Simone didn't drink, that their children reported in to them every hour while everyone else's ran loose around the neighborhood, stopping at various houses to eat the leftovers, the older ones sneaking beer out of coolers, or bottles off of backyard bars, like scavengers. Elise's daughter, Mona, was thirteen. She was an only child, and Elise imagined she was home with her book, an old, musty copy of *Jane Eyre*, avoiding the events as was her custom, fixing herself meals from their kitchen, and hiding upstairs when the neighbors reached their house, a little after three o'clock. By that time, a lull had been reached. At Elise and Will's, the events, somehow, had to regenerate. Elise did not know how this happened, but it always did. Some alchemy occurred—the way the sun hit the back patio, or shone off the black-bottomed pool, the pitchers of sangria they served, the desire to be immersed in water at the moment they lacked the power to refuse themselves. Each year, like a welcoming enticement, the pool held a splattering of violet jacaranda petals. The men swam stripped to the waist. A few of the women, like Gina Beldon, swam in their lingerie.

The same old stories took on a freshness in the presence of the newcomers, and inevitably the story of the nighttime swimmers came out. It was the most popular, and each year Elise suffered through it. She found, from the first, that she could not walk away from the tellers, that listening to it became a kind of blunt self-torture. The story was most often retold at the Millers'. It was Josie Miller who had actually seen two people in her pool. But since the house was vacated, for sale, and Josie had moved into her parents' house in the Isles, it came up at Elise and Will's, just as most people were emerging from the water, the women draping themselves in towels, the men standing in their own puddles, wetting their cigarettes with damp fingers.

This year, Simone and Doug listened, rapt. The swimmers had been spotted in the Millers' pool the night before the Memorial Day events. It had been two a.m. and Josie had been up, making her lobster dip.

"I wasn't drunk, I swear to you," Josie originally told the group. And now, someone made her declaration for her. She wasn't drunk, they said. She swore it. She heard the noise of the splashing, a small sound, but something that made her stop what she was doing. It was a woman's laugh beneath the splashing that intrigued her enough to investigate. The Millers' pool was several feet from the house. It was surrounded by tropicals that blocked anyone's view of the water, especially at night when the pool lights weren't lit. But Josie crept up and peered through the bamboo. There had been a man and a woman, clearly without clothes. In an embrace, she added. With their hair wet, and slicked back, she couldn't tell who they were. At this point she told of stumbling back and sprawling into the landscaped bed, and admitted, maybe one or two martinis had entered her bloodstream. Usually, the crowd groaned and disbelieved her.

This year, Elise found it sad listening to the story told without her. She missed Josie's exaggerated features, her long nose, her bright fingernails against the glass in her hand. No one else seemed to mind. When Josie regained her position, someone said, the swimmers had disappeared. Simone and Doug, arms linked, laughed together. They looked at each other as if they'd been put on. But no, Will insisted, picking up the story, his voice's enthusiasm draining Elise of strength, they were heard in other pools throughout the night. And then people spoke up, almost everyone attesting to having heard splashing, high-pitched laughing, even muffled shrieks and moans. Josie was always vindicated by scores of neighborhood witnesses. The swimmers had made a night of it, sex in every pool, as impossible and far-fetched as that seemed.

The first year Elise and Will had moved to the neighborhood, the Memorial Day events were already in place. They were the newcomers then and the swimmers had not yet made their appearance. Standing around one of the pools, Elise had been young and drunk. She wore a Lilly Pulitzer sundress. She had her hair long and straight and clipped back on the sides with barrettes. They had moved to Florida from Massachusetts, a relocation that made her feel alien in the strange heat, her clothes damp, her hair suddenly buoyant with humidity. The year before, playing badminton in the soft grass of their old backyard, she would not have known herself standing by this pool, a drink in her hand, her two-year-old tended by a neighbor's teenage daughter. The house hopping had reminded her of something, and she spoke up, spurred by the drink, an old-fashioned made for her by a man who stood beside her, the soft hair on his arm brushing her elbow, the residue of his cologne caught somehow on her own skin.

Had anyone seen the movie *The Swimmer*? she'd asked. A few people shrugged, slightly interested. "With Burt Lancaster," she said. "All wet and dripping, in skimpy trunks?" She failed in her attempt to explain the plot to them. It was all too confusing, with the drinks, and the man's arm and his hand then, touching her elbow. She felt herself lean into him. Will had somehow disappeared. Someone asked her when the movie had come out, and she explained that it was old, that she had seen it as a child in a Sheraton Hotel in Boston. Her parents had gone out and she had woken up alone in the middle of the night and to pass the time turned on the television. Her story was met with the quiet, unacknowledged space of polite distance, soft smiles, and people turning away to start up with someone else.

Elise saw now that none of their parents ever left them alone in hotel rooms, that the shock of this admission was enough to overshadow her mention of the movie. None of them ever remembered she'd brought it up. She had not explained to anyone at the time that later in college she'd read the Cheever story on which the movie had been based, and in it she had seen her whole life mirrored—her father's alcoholism, his debt, the house lost when she was sixteen. Instead, she had told that to the man whose fingers held her elbow, lightly, like a benediction or a salve. He had kissed her then, too, leading her first into a small room she thought now had been a pantry, with its smells of boxed sweetened cereals and onions in netted bags, but at the time she hadn't cared, his mouth and the sense of loss surpassing the surprise of infidelity. His name was Joe Trevor. She discovered this pushing Mona in her stroller days later, past the Capes and Colonials she only vaguely remembered visiting. He came out of a yellow Cape with green shutters. It was late afternoon. He wore a dress shirt and a loosened tie, and he called her name.

"Joe Trevor?" he said, stepping quickly down the length of his driveway. And then, "You've forgotten me already."

She had been forced to slow and then stop. "No," she said. She looked into his face, which seemed disappointed. His eyebrows and hair were dark. His eyes were blue, flashing something at her. They stood in the tree shade that covered the street. Mona sat obediently in her stroller, her little hands knotted together.

"Well then," he said. His eyes kept up their secret.

"Yes?" she said. She would not be the first one to say it, that she wanted to fall into his arms.

"When can I see you?" he asked.

She caught her breath. She looked up and down the street, but they were alone.

"I have no idea," she said. She felt her mouth tremble. She moved her hair from her face.

He stood there, looking at her, watching her mouth, her hand moving up.

"Yes you do," he said, relentless. "When?"

She sighed. Would there have been a point in denying herself? She looked down at the pavement. Her hair fell over her face again. "All right," she said, resigned. Will often worked late. The babysitter was always available. She looked up at him, and he seemed happier, relieved even. They set a time and place. She had not felt any guilt, just an overwhelming need for him to touch her, which he would time and again for a year in a motel room off the Causeway. Near the end they had gotten careless. In the afternoons while Mona napped he would slip through the backyards to her house. She would let him in the back gate by the pool. They would swim afterward, warily, though the neighbors on both sides of Elise worked. And once, Mona woke up. She came quietly, unnoticed, to the sliding glass doors. Elise was kissing Joe Trevor on the pool steps. Their bodies had been bare and wet and pressed together. Elise had felt Mona's eyes on her and she glanced up to meet her daughter's gaze through the glass, a look of gentle surprise on her pink-cheeked face, something disarming in her expression.

Forever afterward Elise feared Mona would let something slip. Elise knew Mona hadn't understood what she'd seen, but she worried that later the memory would surface at a time when she might. She had held her daughter at arm's length. She had watched her grow up with an unconscious trepidation, the two of them coolly polite. Mona always knocked loudly on her mother's bedroom door. In the afternoons she would ring the bell to be let in the house after school. She was tall and well developed for her age, and her shyness lent her an aloof appeal that attracted the boys in the neighborhood. They came to the door sweaty after baseball to ask for her. She glared at them from the stair landing.

"What?" she would ask, her irritation overcoming her shyness.

They grinned at her, speechless. Mona would turn and retreat up the stairs, leaving them gaping and awkward, tugging on the fronts of their T-shirts. Now, standing in the large circle of neighbors by her pool, Elise noticed the teenagers gathering along the edges of the yards, the boys' legs bony in long shorts, the girls' shirts stretched across their small breasts. Among the group were Joe Trevor's children, the ones he returned to after only two months of separation from his wife. He had missed the way she made his toast, the solid line of shoes in his closet, the balled socks in his bureau drawer, the yard tools marked with the sweat of his hands. Elise did not fault him his choice. At the time, she could not have decided herself what she was willing to compromise. Across the pool Joe Trevor stood under the jacaranda, still happily unsatisfied eleven years later, married to the woman he had once denounced. Of Elise's presence he had remained faithfully oblivious.

The switch to the next house was never signaled by anyone in particular. Small groups decided among themselves, and the general pattern, the swigging down of drinks, the trickling of people through the pool gate, became the sign to move on. Today, Elise found she could not. She lingered, pretending to clean up.

She had done this that second year, waiting for a word from Joe Trevor, for him to slip back in through the gate and face her. The sun was low behind the house. The pool, in the shadow, gave its bottomless effect. Elise poured herself another drink. He had not come then, of course. She recalled her belief that he might and saw it now as childish, somehow selfish. Beyond the pool gate she watched the teenagers on the lawn under the somber shade of live oaks, hands clutched, palms pressed to the small of bare backs. The coming evening smelled of mown grass and the smoke of their covert cigarettes. Elise felt the stir of their bodies, their eagerness, like an injury.

The evening progressed. Nothing occurred out of the ordinary. One of the children was pushed into a pool and four men dove fully clothed to save him, only to have him surface and swim, expertly, to the side. Gina Beldon's husband slipped and cut his lip on his glass of bourbon. He had been tended by sober Simone, on her knees with a compress, and driven by Doug to the emergency room for stitches. Elise had envied Simone's fluid movements, her unhampered judgment. The moon came out, nearly full and luminous. Children who had been pedaling their bikes, playing manhunt in the maze of yards, had put themselves to bed. Neighbors began to wander home, shadowy shapes meandering the neighborhood streets, still clutching wine goblets. Elise and Will lingered. Neither of them looked forward to returning home, their silence so vastly different from the blur of noise and distraction they had just experienced, but they finally headed toward the street, the pavement slanting up to meet Elise's every step, Will disgruntled, unhappy about the night's end.

Suddenly he stopped and reached for her hand. "Let's go swimming," he said. His face was white and shining in the moonlight.

"You're drunk," she told him, and continued walking.

"You can't stand me," he said then, refusing to keep step with her, hanging back and waiting for her to stop.

She turned and looked at him. She could make out only the bright material of his shirt. She did not feel like arguing.

"That's it, then," he said. His voice sounded plaintive. Elise did not want to placate him, but she knew from experience that she must.

"Of course not," she said. "I've never heard anything so silly."

"Say you love me," Will said.

Elise felt as if a hole had opened in the pavement beneath her. She felt her body plunged, roughly, into its depths.

"I love you," she said, the words dry and tired on her lips.

She continued walking, leaving him behind with what he thought he wanted, which she knew would not be enough. Their house stood back from the road, its walkway lined with tiny lanterns, flanked by two oaks whose limbs' wrenching shape framed the upper story. At one time she had wondered what she ever needed beyond the bay windows neatly curtained, the carpeted stairs, the slate hallways. The Royal Doulton, and her mother's silver saved from the bankruptcy, the acquired antique furniture with its smell of an old parlor. There was the new GE washer and dryer, the cleansers for every surface, the pantry filled with J&B and Schmirnoff, with duck pâté, with assorted breakfast cereals and packaged rice and artificial mashed potatoes. In the attic was Mona's old high chair, her infant blanket, Elise's cocktail dresses, worn once and discarded. Wasn't all of this, she had thought, part of love? Wasn't love part of this?

Inside, the house was chilled and dark. She did not remember removing her clothes, or if she had checked on Mona, or if Will had ever come inside. Much later, she was awakened by something, and waited in the dark of the bedroom to determine what it had been. A noise, she thought. Outside. Will's form in the bed was a shadowy mound, distinguished by his breathing and its monotony. She went downstairs, gripping the banister, to the sliding glass doors. The pool lights were lit, and Elise saw Mona and a neighborhood boy in the water. His hair was wet and swiped back. His shoulders were tanned and narrow. Mona wore her blue swimsuit, the straps tied around her neck, her own shoulders rounded and soft. They stood facing each other, and then the boy disappeared beneath the surface, and Mona made a small noise, one she tried to muffle with a hand over her mouth, her eyes casting up toward Elise's bedroom window.

Elise did not stay at the glass door. She went up to the bedroom and lay back on the bed. She did not try to sleep. She listened to Will's steady breath. She remembered the night she and Joe Trevor had become notorious. It had been her idea to swim the pools of the neighborhood. She and Joe had been in bed in his hotel room, the one he took after he left his wife. The sheets had been damp and twisted, wrung out under their bodies. There had been a high, elated sense of hopefulness between them. He had agreed to her plan, laughing, holding her down on the bed. Elise knew she had to leave soon to pick up something for dinner. She had asked him to kiss her, and he had moved toward her and said, "Anything."

They met at one a.m. in the Barringtons' side yard. The Barringtons had the largest pool, a long, classic shape with geraniums in concrete urns at each corner. The rim of the pool was decorated with Spanish mosaic tile. The night's heat held them in a damp fist. The geraniums shed their red petals on the white deck. They wore bathing suits at first. But once in the water, their hands on each other, feeling the slide of skin, the fit of their legs under the surface, they had taken them off. They had not really bothered to swim the pool's length. They deviated from the story in this respect. And they had not, as was believed, swum in all of the pools, only the Barringtons', where they had lingered for an hour or so, and then the Millers', where they had been observed.

Joe wasn't worried about being seen. He had wanted to go on to the next pool, but Elise had not dared. They left each other under the cover of the Millers' backyard trellis. She moved quickly across her own lawn, past the line of tiny lanterns lining the walk, and into her house. She had changed and slipped into bed, her skin smelling of chlorine, her hair leaving a wet mark on the pillow. She had tried to slow her breathing. She had been beset with joy. She imagined Joe behind the wheel of his car driving back to the hotel sheets still smelling of her skin, the hands that had held her now wrapped around the wheel, his expression happy and satisfied. But she had been wrong. She no longer tried to imagine what he might have been feeling. He had shown up at the Memorial Day events at his wife's side, surprising Elise. All day she had tried to catch him alone, but he had persisted in avoiding her, in giving her silent pleas a sorrowful shake of the head that ended everything.

Downstairs, she heard Mona come through the sliding door. She heard her footfalls on the stairs, her furtive movements beyond the bedroom walls. Elise rose and went into her daughter's room. She flipped the switch and the room sharpened with light. Mona feigned sleep, her bathing suit wetting the carpet at the foot of the bed, her book abandoned on the white painted desk. Elise did not know what she intended. She went to the window and gripped the sill. Below her the pool water still wavered clear and incandescent. She remembered the promise of the water rising up her thighs, the skimming of the surface, her arms and legs loosening, her hair fanning out. He had held her face in his hands. There was the small scar on his forearm. His eyes with their expectancy. She wound her legs about his waist. The water rolled down the curve of his throat. His hands traced their usual route. Around the perimeter moths fluttered like mouths meeting light. In her daughter's bedroom, exposed in the glare, Elise rushed to the bed and stumbled and bumped her leg. The pain moved up and down her shin like a caress. She sank onto the mattress and reached out and gave Mona's shoulders a little shake.

"You saw us," she said. She heard her voice catch. "Weren't we happy?"

She felt her daughter's quickened heart, soft and trapped beneath the pale sheet. Mona gazed back, her eyes wide and tremulous. The only witness.

Stillborn

They moved into the dead woman's house in August. First the woman's husband who had kept bees died, and then a year later the woman had followed. Diana heard this from the white-haired neighbor the first time they visited the property. The house was reached by a narrow, unpaved lane flanked by old beeches grown close together. At the end of the lane was Long Island Sound, a gray expanse, dotted on windy days with white caps. The house backed up to the salt marsh, and from the upstairs window Diana could see across the blowing grasses to a row of painted cottages like a colorful necklace. Their new address was Edge Lea. She was six months into her pregnancy, and the house, a rambling clapboard cottage, felt calm and empty. They'd wait until after the baby to paint the beadboard walls and redo the kitchen. For now they would simply take down the ramp leading up to the front door. In the end it seemed the dead woman's husband had needed a wheelchair. The ramp was made of heavy pine planks that took a day's work to pull away. Diana's husband yanked at the rusted nails with a hammer, sweating and cursing, swatting at the bees bobbing about his head and shoulders.

Inside the house Diana found an empty Ponds Cold Cream container high up on the linen closet shelf. It was milk glass, the kind of thing she might have hidden small treasures in as a child. She set it on the window ledge above the sink. Diana was not the type to hum or sing aloud to herself, but she found it natural to do so here in the dead woman's house. Maybe it was the woman's spirit, she thought. She wasn't concerned or frightened by the thought of interference by the dead woman's spirit. She sang songs from old Broadway musicals like *Oklahoma*—"I'm just a girl who can't say no, I'm in a terrible fix!"—and songs from her elementary school music book—"Oh Señor Don Gato was a cat, on a high red roof Don Gato sat." Her husband came in from working outside with a bee sting on his forearm.

"You can't swat at them," she said. "Bees sting in defense."

He gave her one of his looks. His lip curled up. She loved that look, and loved provoking it. She took him under the chin and shook his face back and forth. "He went there to read a letter, Meow meow meow, Where the reading light was better, Meow meow meow, 'Twas a love note for Don Gato!"

Her husband put his dirty hands on her stomach, distended and hard like a medicine ball. The baby shifted and pressed her little foot up. "Oh!" she said. "She's telling you to back off, buster."

Her husband smiled, hesitantly. "*Buster*?" he said.

"I don't know," she said. "I don't know where that came from."

"Your mother?" he said. "Did your mother ever say that word?"

"The movie," she said. "The last one we watched."

At night they sat on their new couch and watched Alfred Hitchcock movies, one after the other, and ate long sticks of licorice. She was annoyed. Her husband considered her mother cheap and uneducated. His fear that she would become a woman like her mother was something he'd never admit. "My mother would never say *buster*," she said. "Not seriously."

"Maybe she should. It's better than a lot of other words she's used," he said. He went to the sink to wash his hands. On her white shirt he'd left the imprints of his fingers.

In September the few summer people had gone. Diana decided to plant bulbs along the back of the house—daffodils and allium, hyacinth and crocus. It had grown cold at night, and the wind came off the salt marsh, rushed up the narrow lane from the Sound. The house groaned and rattled. The rows of trees grew bright, as if electrified. There was cold rain, and the leaves came down into the dead yard, pretty and wet. She bought the bulbs and began to dig with her trowel. "Chicks and ducks and geese better scurry, when I take you out in my surrey, when I take you out in my surrey with the fringe on top!" She sang softly, and dug around with her trowel, and uncovered a small bone, then another. *Femur, fibula, humerus, clavicle.* Tiny bones, delicate and dirt-stained. She stopped digging, the bones uncovered. I've dug too deep, she thought. She leaned onto the side of the house and pulled herself upright. The sky was dotted with swirling leaves. The marsh grass filled with wind. She stood for a long time look-ing down at the upturned earth, and her hand holding the trowel shook. Her husband was at work, teaching at the university. She went to the neighbor Mrs. Merrick's house and knocked. The old woman lived at the end of the lane in a wood-shingled cottage on a bluff overlooking the rocky shore. She came to the door, her white hair long and loose past her shoulders.

"What is it?" she asked, sharply. Diana imagined she thought it was the baby, and she didn't want to be burdened.

"Something in the garden," she said.

The two of them walked back down the gravel lane, and Diana pointed toward the spot. Mrs. Merrick went over and looked down. She had on leather shoes, plaid slacks, a wool sweater. The wind lifted the strands of her white hair. She bent lower and then stood up and looked back at Diana. "It's the stillborn," she said, flatly. Her face seemed deflated, the skin sagging around her mouth. She kicked the pile of dirt back over the spot with her shoe, and then she came over to Diana and took her arm. Diana allowed herself to be led back inside her own house. Mrs. Merrick boiled water for tea. Outside the sky was blue and white and riddled with leaves.

"What were you doing digging there?" the woman said. She searched through Diana's cabinets for cups, for the tea.

"I was just planting bulbs," she said.

"Those go in the front, not the back."

"How was I supposed to know?" Diana cried. She had her hands placed on the mound of her stomach.

Mrs. Merrick's face softened. She took out the good china cups and saucers. "Don't go worrying. It was years ago that baby was buried. Before you were born."

The dead woman whose house they lived in had given birth to four children. The stillborn baby was her third. "A wisp of a thing, not full term," Mrs. Merrick said. She blew on her tea. Her hair was still disordered from the wind. Diana stared at her tea-cup. Mrs. Merrick got a faraway look. "It wasn't unheard of. She had other babies to tend, and she knew there'd be more, and it was done. The husband took the shovel. Not sure how so much of the soil could have washed away, but that must be the reason you uncovered it. No stone or marker. Just up near the house there where you dug."

The woman took a loud sip of the tea. She eyed Diana. "Drink it."

Diana imagined she had stepped into a fairy tale. This was the witch, the tea spiked with henbane, the ground littered with dead children. Her baby did a spin—*back handspring*, her husband would have said. *Our little gymnast*, he called her. She reached for the tea, and her hand still shook.

"No marker? Nothing?"

Mrs. Merrick scoffed. "The baby never drew a breath. Now I hear in the hospitals they have special nurses, and grief counselors, and they let the parents and the family members hold the baby and put clothes on it. They bring in photographers and take pictures even."

Diana couldn't tell what Mrs. Merrick thought about all of these new developments, whether they were a waste of time, whether grief was something best dealt with alone.

"Was she sad?" Diana asked.

"Sure, I'm sure she was. Carried the baby for nearly seven months. Must have felt something—useless, tired, guilty. All sorts of things you feel."

Diana sipped the tea, uneasy. She kept seeing the bones.

"Your milk comes in and there's no child to nurse. You flatten out and there's always something that was supposed to be there, after all that—swollen feet, and various discomforts."

Mrs. Merrick put her cup noisily into the saucer. She stood up and placed both in the kitchen sink. She walked carefully, favoring one hip. Her plaid pants sagged in the rear. Diana watched her walk to the door. "You'll be fine," the woman said. She opened the kitchen door and the wind nearly grabbed it from her hand. She turned back.

"Bulbs go in the front of the house," she said. "Looks pretty. First thing you see when you come home."

And then she was gone.

Diana didn't tell her husband about the bones in the garden, or what would have been the garden, if she'd ever planted the bulbs, which she did not. She hid them in the crawl space under the porch in their little boxes. Her husband would have called the authorities, let them take the bones and examine them and launch an investigation. Mrs. Merrick would be contacted to give testimony, and Diana knew she'd be disgruntled, called upon to talk about something already over and done with. The dead woman's remaining children, scattered around the country with their own families, might not have known they had another sibling. Diana felt she had disturbed enough. Now when she saw Mrs. Merrick at the A&P, the woman steered her shopping cart close and reached out and gave Diana's hand a squeeze. It was their secret.

In late October, the sun dull and low over the salt marsh, the marsh grass flattened from frost, Mrs. Merrick came to Diana's door. She carried a small wicker basket. Diana saw her from the window in the upstairs hall—the wind flapping her coat, her hair held back with a scarf like the kind the women in the Hitchcock films wore when they went for drives in convertibles. When Diana opened the door, Mrs. Merrick stepped inside quickly, covertly, as if she were being followed. She smelled of cloves.

"I've baked you something," she said.

She set the basket down on the kitchen table and took out a loaf of pumpkin bread.

Diana thought of food carried in baskets, wolves watching from the woods. "Oh, how nice," she said. The baby was large and sluggish these days. Diana always felt as if she might topple over. Her back ached. She spent a lot of time trying to nap.

"I didn't wake you, did I?" Mrs. Merrick said. "I won't keep you."

Diana insisted she stay. "We'll have tea," she said. She went to the cabinet, but Mrs. Merrick told her to sit, and she'd get it ready. And like the last time, she set out the china cups and started the water to boil. She sat down at the table with Diana and scanned the kitchen, the room beyond.

"It seems so empty," she said. "Nice and neat, though."

"Did they have a lot of furniture?" Diana asked.

"Oh, too much," Mrs. Merrick said. "And then they had things on shelves and tabletops, stacked in corners. All sorts of odds and ends. Collecting dust."

The kettle boiled and she rose to pour the water into the teapot. "Once the children were grown and gone it seems the things took their place." She looked at Diana as she set the teapot on the table. "Things never take the place of people in my book, but for some they do."

"What sorts of things did they have?"

"Oh, books and magazines and knickknacks—collections of things—buttons, china, shells, even taxidermy creatures—chipmunks and birds and the like."

Diana thought again about the bones. Maybe they were just the bones of some little animal. She could have been wrong.

34

"Like the Nut Lady?" Diana asked. "Was it like that?"

The Nut Lady, Mrs. Tashjian, lived near Diana when she was a child. Her old house was the Nut Museum, and admission was one nut. Diana's mother would send her to the door with food—CorningWare dishes filled with casseroles—and Diana would duck beneath the overgrown trees and ring the bell, the casserole warm in her hands. The woman, stooped and bright-eyed, had a singsongy voice. Behind her the house was dark, and somewhere were displays of her collection of nuts and nut art, and squirrels running up and down the grand staircase, and cobwebs, and damp plaster. Diana wouldn't go in, even though the woman asked her to. "My mother is waiting," she'd say, and point to her mother's car idling under the tree canopy. Later, after the woman was taken to the home, and the house was sold, and the trees were cut down, Diana always wished she had gone inside, just once.

"They were eccentric," Mrs. Merrick said. "Everyone has their own obsessions."

"Did you know them well? Did you know them when she had the baby?"

Mrs. Merrick looked at her over her teacup. Her eyes were the palest blue that Diana had ever seen, as if their color had washed away.

"I was a girl," she said. "About sixteen."

"Did you ever help her with the other children?" Diana asked.

Mrs. Merrick set her cup down carefully on the saucer. "Of course I was a help in those days. I cared for them all—Elizabeth and Matthew and Nancy. They were good babies. Good children."

"But she never considered a name? In all the time she carried her?"

Outside the wind picked up and a tree branch made a grating sound against the house.

"You should cut that back," Mrs. Merrick said. She stood up, supporting her weight with a hand on the tabletop. She took the basket. "Time I should go."

Diana walked her to the door. The baby moved, a slow roll from one side to the other. She pressed her hand there, and Mrs. Merrick watched her, her pale eyes impossible to read. She opened the door and the salt air blew through, flapping the appointment slips and advertisements stuck to the refrigerator.

"Iris," she said. She turned and looked at Diana. "That was the name she was thinking for her."

Like the bulb, Diana thought. She nodded. "It's pretty," she said.

"What name have you settled on?" Mrs. Merrick asked.

Diana smiled. "Oh, I like Madeleine," she said. "But my husband wants Katherine, for his grandmother."

Mrs. Merrick smiled. Her eyes flashed. "You carry her, you name her." She slipped her scarf over her head and tied the ends under her chin. Diana watched her walk down the lane toward her house. The Sound beyond was alive with little darting waves.

That night Diana told her husband she wanted the baby to be named Madeleine.

"I've thought it over," she said.

He looked at her askance over his laptop. "I thought we said we'd see if she looked like a Madeleine or a Katherine once she was here."

Diana lay out on the couch with her feet up. She put her hand on the mound of her stomach. "She's already *here*," she said. "And she seems to me to be a Madeleine."

Her husband gave her a look then. Not the look she liked, but one she'd never seen. She didn't know why she was insisting on a name, and she regretted it now that she saw his expression—one of betrayal, and confusion. *Who are you?* his face said.

In November she found the postcard. She'd been pulling out the drawers built into the wall of book shelves. One held a matchbook from Hundred Acres, a restaurant that had been closed for years. She was curious about the dead woman. She admitted to herself that she was looking for something. The postcard depicted a painted image of the entrance to another private beach off of Shore Road, less than a mile away. The postage date was August 5, 1959, and it was addressed to Arlene Guernsey. *Wish you were here*, the message said. It was signed, *Charlie Warlie*, with a slanted, messy hand, in pencil. Diana held the postcard to the window to read it in the light. She knew the dead woman's name was Arlene, she'd seen it on the papers at the closing—Arlene Whitcomb Life Trust. Whitcomb was her married name. Her husband had been Roy. Mrs. Merrick had said it herself—"Oh, Roy was the most patient man," she'd said. "Patient and long-suffering." Diana had thought she meant *suffering* in the physical sense, but now she wondered if his wife had been cheating, and his *suffering* had been of another kind.

That afternoon Diana's husband called to tell her he was going to New York.

"I'm taking the train," he said.

Diana felt a little put out. She'd wanted to talk to him about Charlie Warlie and Arlene. She wanted company, and it was so close to her due date.

"Why are you going?" she said. "What if I go into labor?"

Her husband sighed. "The baby isn't due for a few weeks." He didn't explain why he was going, and Diana didn't ask. It was always something for school—meetings, and readings, and conferences. She was used to his traveling. It was something she wasn't supposed to question.

"Fine," she said. "I can always call Mrs. Merrick."

There was a silence on the line—a little pause. "Who?"

"Our neighbor," she said. "Down the lane."

"Oh, yes," he said. "Or your mother." Then he laughed, as if both of these solutions were nonsensical. "You just call the doctor and a cab. That will get you to the hospital in plenty of time."

"And what about you?" she asked.

"Of course you call me," he said. "I'll be there in plenty of time, too."

That night the wind and rain came at the house in gusts. Diana heard one of the shutters bang and then make a sound as if it'd been wrenched from the house. Blustery, she thought. She'd remembered yet another song from her childhood—"Early one morning, just as the sun was rising, I heard a maiden sing in the valley below"—and she sang it out loud into the dark room. The baby was moving, and she sang the song to her and imagined that when she was born she would remember it. Eerie, lilting melodies were always memory triggers in old movies. Then there was another sharp banging noise, and Diana felt suddenly cold. The baby stilled, as if listening with her. She didn't want to investigate the noise, but she felt she must. She eased herself to the end of the bed and stood. She felt a funny twisting feeling, a little cramp. "Oh," she thought. But it was nothing. The noise came again, and Diana leaned on the banister as she went downstairs. In the living room she could hear the noise, constant now, a sort of hurried, urgent knocking. She went to the kitchen door and peered out. The porch light illuminated a small patch of grass below the steps, and there was Mrs. Merrick turning away. She had on a dark slicker, but Diana saw her white head when the hood blew back. She saw her gnarled hands yank the hood back on. And then she was gone around the house. Diana didn't open the door and call for her. It was too strange, Mrs. Merrick being there at this hour in the storm. Diana went around to the front of the house and peered out of the living room window, and there was Mrs. Merrick heading back down the lane. She had a flashlight, and the light cast its narrow beam, filled with spikes of rain. The slicker blew around her like a dark orb.

Ava Merrick had long suffered her name. She had the dark hair, the lush mouth of Ava Gardner, and boys would always find some comparison, and girls always hated her. She'd taken Lizzie and Matthew down to dig clams. Mrs. Guernsey had been home with the baby. It helped that this was a small shore community, that the summer people left, always a blessing, that quiet stretch of fall and winter, into spring. It was late summer then, only a few families lingered—the Norths, the Skeltons. There were two boys about her age who went about together, and they appeared at the end of the beach and approached her.

"Ave Maria," one said. "It's Ava."

She ignored them, and continued to wade into the water, digging with her toes. Lizzie plopped a clam in the bucket, and a boy leaned over to look. Lizzie beamed at him. Matthew was more hesitant—a timid seven-year-old. He stood by his sister like a protector.

"You've got some," the boy said, the rakish one with sun-bleached hair, Howard Skelton.

He grinned at the children, as if he were a nice boy. Ava knew he was not, that this was a ruse. Still, she ignored him.

"What about you?" he asked Ava. He waded over to her to look into her bucket. His fingers slid along the rim and then slid up along her waist.

Ava stepped away from his hand. His friend, Will North, laughed. Once Will had come upon her reading and sat down beside her in the sand and touched her breast, as if she were an item in a store to be perused. She didn't say anything about any of this to her father. Her mother was dead, and there were no women to confess to other than Mrs. Guernsey, and Mrs. Guernsey was busy, always busy with the children, the baby, the house, the garden. At night in her bed she would relive these incidents, and though her face burned with shame from the memories, she found she also got a sharp pleasure from them. When Mr. Guernsey, Roy, took her with the children to the movies in Niantic and placed his hand on her leg in the dark, Ava was prepared to feel both the shame and the pleasure.

He approached her one morning soon after on the beach. He was dressed in his work pants, his button-down shirt. His forehead was high, his hair thinning and fair. Ava had never seen him on the beach in the morning. She watched his leather soles slipping, and imagined his shoes filling with sand.

"Just the girl I've been looking for," he said. The wind and the water seemed to take his voice.

Ava looked up at him. "Is everything all right?"

Nancy had come down with a fever the day before, and they suspected bronchitis. Ava's childhood friend had died of pneumonia, and she'd sat with her holding her hot hand, the whole time thinking she'd get well. She was worrying about Nancy, her little flushed face and the cough, when Roy wrapped his long arm around her shoulders and steered her toward the path that wound up through the stones to her house. Ava feared the worst—Nancy taken to the hospital, the news broken to her by Mr. Guernsey in the kindest of ways. She'd be needed at the house to watch the children while they sat by Nancy's bedside. She was thinking about all of this when they came to the door of her house.

"It's Nancy, isn't it?" she said.

Roy Guernsey opened the door and led her inside. He was flushed, breathing heavily, and Ava had a moment of fear that he had gotten ill himself. But no, he had tugged her toward his chest and put his hands in her hair and then slid them down her back, pressing and kneading, his mouth moving to her neck and then, with an awful groan, to her mouth. Ava's father had gone to work. It was a workday, after all. Ava hadn't forgotten the movie theater, but she hadn't expected that what happened there would lead to this sort of violence. He'd dragged her down onto the floor. Her head hit the leg of the armchair, but he didn't notice. She heard his belt buckle fall to the floor beside her, felt the weight of him, and then his sharp entry—a knifelike searing. He panted and moaned and then made a sound like a high wail. All of it, even the pain, thrilled her. She'd watched his face the whole time—his eyes squeezed tight like Matthew's when she took out a splinter. His flyaway hair, the sheen of his pate, the long, dignified nose. Her body felt the heat of his, the damp between them becoming wet. He'd fumbled with her shirt, with the catch to her bra, and when it came free he'd sighed and nuzzled his mouth there like a baby. He tugged at her pants and slid his mouth down, and she watched the top of his head in surprise, the way it dipped and bobbed. Beyond the surprise she felt nothing the first time.

They lay in a heap of clothing on the living room floor. The light came in and the rushing sound of the tide hitting the rocks. He curled beside her and kissed her and said her name over and over, as if he were practicing it. He was like a small boy after, tender and sweet. She put her hand on his cheek, on the fine stubble of his chin that had made the skin around her mouth burn. She didn't remember what she said. Then he was up, telling her to dress, telling her he would see her again soon.

"You understand what this means?" he said.

Ava had stared at him, buttoning her blouse. The house in its disorder humiliated her—the clutter of her father's collections, the pile of laundry on the sofa, the mess in the kitchen she'd not yet cleaned up.

"We're lovers," he said. "Secret lovers."

When fall came, and school, Ava would babysit at the Guernseys' in the afternoons, and Roy would come in from work and loosen his tie and pour a drink and watch her. She would pretend nothing was different, but the children knew.

"Why is your face red?" Lizzie would ask. She'd put her two hands on Ava's cheeks to feel for a fever. Ava would take the children out on the windy beach, and Roy would come and walk along beside her and whisper to her. "Stay home tomorrow," he'd say. "Tell your father you're sick."

Ava had been a good student and hated missing school, but she was also dutiful and desirous and she would pretend she had a sore throat, or a headache, or women's trouble, and her father would grudgingly leave her, and tell her to call Mrs. Guernsey for anything. As soon as he left, Roy arrived. He'd yank off his shirt, unbuckle his belt. They'd taken to using her bedroom at the front of the house, where the sea seemed about to break in through the windows, and the glass was salt-stained, and the gulls looped and sang. Back then there weren't manuals or magazines that talked about how to please men, but Ava knew now that she pleased him by instinct, by watching his face, listening to the noises he made, his body a map, a gridded space where she might place her mouth, her hands. When she soothed the children to sleep she would slowly drag her fingernails up and down their backs, and Roy Guernsey shuddered and sighed when she did this to him, straddling his legs. She wouldn't say now that she loved Roy. They rarely talked about themselves, and she was aware that love had more to do with the sort of closeness that talking revealed, but at the time she knew nothing about that. He would send her little notes, folded into small squares he pressed into her hand when he saw her: *Tomorrow*, the note might say. Sometimes: *Wednesday*.

One day after school Mrs. Guernsey stopped her in front of the house and asked her to come inside. She wore a stained apron, and her hair fell about her face, loosened from a soft bun. She looked drawn and thin, but still beautiful in a way that made Ava, with her rounded limbs and broad shoulders, feel awkward. Mrs. Guernsey took her into the kitchen and handed her a bottle of Lydia Pinkham's tablets.

"Your father says you've got women's issues?" she said.

Ava had seen the ads in the newspaper—accompanied by a woman's face in distress:

Too Worn-Out to Go? Another date broken . . . Couldn't stay on her feet a minute longer! Lydia E. Pinkham's Vegetable Compound always relieves cramps. Try it next month.

Or:

"Please Let Me Alone!" Out of sorts . . . disagreeable! Lydia E. Pinkham's Vegetable Compound has helped so many women whose nerves are frayed by those dreadful "monthly" headaches.

She took the pill bottle and looked at the label.

"Don't be embarrassed," Mrs. Guernsey said. "These will help."

Years later Ava learned that the tablets were taken by desperate barren women hoping to induce pregnancy. "A Baby in Every Bottle," Mrs. Pinkham claimed. She had never taken the pills; the bottle still sat in her medicine cabinet. When Mrs. Guernsey handed them to her, she hadn't gotten her period for two months, and hadn't needed them. At first she'd seen it as a relief from the bloody pads. It was Roy who noticed her growing abdomen, whose terrified expression forced her to accept the truth. Still, he passed her the notes, and she met him. He moved his hands over her, enthralled. Everything felt better to her then—she became aroused at the sight of him at the door, and then aroused when he pressed the note into her hand, and then in the days in between she felt overcome and panicked with desire. The pregnancy caused her no trouble at all. She was a big-boned girl and wore loose dresses. She cut slits in her waistbands and wore sweaters and her father's heavy plaid coat in the winter. As the weather grew warmer she wore men's shirts she found at St. Anne's Nearly New shop. It was the style, anyway. She didn't worry about the baby coming. She assumed Roy would tell her what to do. She left it all up to him, despite the way his face became pinched and pale against her pillowcase when, after they were done and lay spent, she placed his hand on the baby moving inside of her.

Of course, she'd had cause to worry. She stood now at her kitchen window and tied a knot in the belt of her heavy sweater. She'd gotten a chill last night. The Sound was still dark, the sky gray from the storm. She couldn't say what sent her out in the rain to Diana's house. The house had been dark, Diana presumably asleep. Roy and Arlene were dead, there was nothing she could do now about the bones. She would bake a cottage pie to take over, her desire to be inside the house again after so long impossible to deny. She told herself it had nothing to do with Diana's baby. She peeled the potatoes, set them to boil.

Diana called her husband's cell and it went to his voice mail. She pressed her hand to her abdomen and heard herself make a sound like a cat's mewl. She tried to sing something, but she had forgotten the words, the melodies. Outside was bitter cold, the wind whipping up what looked like bits of ash, and she didn't want to leave the house. Arlene Guernsey, she determined, had met some man one summer and carried on with him behind her husband's back. She could see from the date on the postcard that she'd already had her children, that she would have had to hire a babysitter to leave the house to meet him—maybe Mrs. Merrick, then a teenager. And there'd been a baby, one conceived from the illicit affair, and the baby was the stillborn, out there in the dirt along the house. Diana felt her pulse race at the thought—the baby hidden away, the hospital, the doctor never consulted. She was sure Mrs. Merrick knew, and she was sure she would drag it out of her. It was only right that she heard the story of the bones on her property.

Her phone rang and it was her husband. "What is it? Why didn't you leave a message?"

"There was a storm," she said. "I thought the house would blow down."

"That house isn't going anywhere," he said. "It's been there for a hundred years."

"And I think I'm in labor," she said. She felt her abdomen tighten again, a long cramp. "I'm going over to Mrs. Merrick's."

"No," he said in what she often called his *stern father* voice. In the background she thought she heard something—a soft question, high-pitched. "Call the doctor. Call the cab."

"I need to ask her something," Diana said. "Who is that there?"

"What do you mean? I'm at a conference. Lots of people are here."

"I mean there with you, in the room."

"Lots of people are here in the room. It's a big room, Diana."

She could tell by the sound of his voice that it was a small room. And there it was, that soft voice again, a laugh. Perhaps it was the television, she thought, and she imagined him in a hotel room, and the television on, maybe an old movie.

"What are you watching?" she said. "Is it Leslie Caron? Oh, not *Gigi*!"

There was a silence, then the sound of rumpled hotel bed sheets. "Diana, I'm not sure what you're talking about. But if you're in labor, if you're *sure*, you need to call the doctor and the cab."

Suddenly she didn't want the doctor, or the cab. Mrs. Merrick knew how to deliver babies. She'd delivered the stillborn, she was sure of it now. If she was going to have her baby she would have it there, in the old house by the sea. She hung up the phone and put on her wool coat and her gloves. She went out the kitchen door and down the lane to the end of the road where Mrs. Merrick's house sat. The wind here was harsh, numbing her face. The tightening in her abdomen had increased. She went up to the front door and used the knocker—oxidized green, shaped like a horse-shoe crab. Mrs. Merrick came immediately. She stared at Diana as if she didn't know who she was. Behind her Diana could see the room—shelves of small posed creatures with threadbare fur, canning jars filled with colorful buttons, with marbles, with sea-washed glass. Diana was looking at the inside of the Guernseys' house, the way Mrs. Merrick had described it. She was suddenly fearful of being invited in, remembering her mother waiting in the car, and the Nut Lady asking her inside. Her mother had been the one who'd known all the words to the show tunes, who'd sung them to Diana as a child. They'd made the casseroles and driven them around to the elderly and unfortunate. Diana remembered the white Skylark with the cloth seats, the casseroles stacked in the back steaming up the interior, her mother flicking her ash out the cracked driver's side window.

Mrs. Merrick promptly shut the door, and in a moment came out in her coat, carrying a covered dish with two pot holders. "I was just heading over to your house," she said, with no other explanation.

Diana looked back down the lane at her house. It seemed

impossibly far. But she turned and the two of them headed in that direction, Mrs. Merrick's gait slow, rolling like a sailor, and Diana reeling from the pain of what must certainly be a contraction. The wind was at their backs, pushing them along.

"Early this year," Mrs. Merrick said, glancing up.

Diana saw that it was snowing—flakes shifting in the wind, settling on the gravel road, on her house's rooftop, on the mailboxes in front of the summer cottages. Inside her house Mrs. Merrick set the casserole on the counter. Diana had questions to ask her, but she couldn't now remember all of them. Her phone was ringing. Diana waved at it. "It's just my husband."

They sat down in their usual spots at the table. The wind rattled the windows.

"You've had a disagreement?" Mrs. Merrick said.

Diana said they had not. She felt incredibly sad, overwhelmed.

"Arlene Guernsey had a lover, didn't she?" she said.

Mrs. Merrick offered no response. She went to the cabinet. "Should we have tea?"

"I found the postcard. Good old Charlie Warlie. And she got pregnant, and the baby was Iris, wasn't it?"

Mrs. Merrick dropped a tea cup into the sink. "Oh dear," she said. "I'm so sorry. It broke."

"Oh for fuck's sake, don't worry about those stupid cups," Diana said. She eased herself out of the chair and leaned on the table. She made a sound that didn't make sense. Her voice seemed unlike her own. She felt an icy rush down her legs and looked to see a puddle widening on the floor.

Mrs. Merrick looked, too. She rubbed her hands on her pants. "You're having your baby," she said. Her blue eyes were darker today, like the Sound. Diana felt she was being tugged along, unbidden, by the course of events.

"There was a girl he was seeing," she said, the shock of the moment compelling her to confess. "Some student. We thought we might make it work. But it won't work, will it?"

Mrs. Merrick said, "Go on and get in bed."

Diana pulled herself up the stairs by the banister. She could hear Mrs. Merrick rummaging around, opening cabinets. She hated her husband, hated his secrecy, his inconstancy. She hated the baby for being his. "I don't care what happens to it once it's out," she called to Mrs. Merrick. "You do whatever you think is best. Take it to the orphanage. Give it to the fairies."

Mrs. Merrick came to the doorway. "Now you're sounding foolish." But Diana saw her smile, a faint movement of her lips.

Ava's baby had come early, her water breaking like Diana's, and pooling on the floor of the kitchen while she scrambled eggs. She'd thrown down a towel and headed up the lane to the Guernseys'. She wasn't thinking clearly, but she wanted to let him know, and what other way was there? She had thought of clever methods—small notes like those he'd written, with the single word *Today*, or the message *It's time*, passed to one of the children and on to him, but in the shock of the moment they appeared to her what they really were—childish, silly. It was midday, a Saturday, and warm, the caretakers out with their buckets of oil paint, freshening up the cottages. She remembered that smell of the paint, would always associate it with that day. It was Arlene who came to the door, and Arlene who suddenly saw what was happening. Arlene with the pale skin, the soft unraveling bun, who sent the children off with her mother, who called Ava's father and said that Ava had gone along to help. They were going to Mystic Seaport and spending the night, she'd said. Her mother was oh-so-happy to have Ava's help, she told him.

At first, Roy did not come into the room where Arlene had taken her. Ava could hear his and Arlene's voices downstairs—Arlene's hushed and questioning, Roy's high-pitched with surprise.

"Who could it have been?" she heard Arlene ask.

"One of those summer boys, maybe the Skelton kid," Roy said. "They were always hanging around."

"She would have been further along," Arlene said.

"Some boy at school then," Roy said.

Ava knew she had made a mistake. Like the notes, the game of it all, the idea that he would accept the baby as his seemed a delusion. She remembered then the tender place where her head had hit the chair leg. She felt that, and more, as the baby forced its way out. Well into the night its head appeared and then slid back, appeared and slid back. Arlene was red with frustration, nearly crying, and Roy was there, his face marked with fear. Arlene had pressed Ava's legs back and ordered her to push. Ava had cried out and told Arlene to get Roy out of the room.

"Now's not the time for modesty," Arlene said. "I need help. Do you want a reputation? Is that what you're after? You're a bad girl, Ava, and you want everyone to know it?"

"I won't push until he goes," she said. "I won't do it."

His face had grown hideous to her, his hands, his long fingers, those of a monster. When the baby finally came, Arlene had wrapped it up and handed it to Roy and he had finally left the room. Ava had cried, shrieking, until Arlene hissed at her to be quiet, and placed her hand over her mouth. The windows had been black, the sea sound very far away, like the sound inside the whelks she held to the children's ears. Ava had slept. The next day her breasts had been heavy, and there was no baby. Arlene had come in to tell her that Roy had taken it to some friends who'd always wanted a child.

"I know you'll be grateful for their kindness," Arlene said. "Later you'll have other children."

But Ava had known that she would not have any other children. "A girl," Arlene had said to Roy when the baby had finally slipped out onto the bed. Ava had opened her eyes, and witnessed the look that passed between them, one of complicity, and fury, and cold acceptance. She had, in the practical way that would be hers for the rest of her life, gone home to the house she shared with her father. She hadn't asked who the people were who had taken her baby, or where they lived. She had imagined, instead, the little girl growing up in a beautiful house with a rose trellis, and a swimming pool, and a bedroom decorated with music boxes and ballerinas, lavished with items a woman who'd yearned for a child for so long might be inclined to purchase. Ava wasn't asked back to the Guernseys'. The children came down to the beach and glanced longingly at Ava's house, but they never came close, and if she happened to come near them out walking, they moved away, as if a punishment lay in store for them if they did not. Roy and Arlene had lived together in the house until their deaths, both of them stony, and unapproachable, even in their later years. Ava had watched Roy tend his bees, the gentle smoke, the white hood, the hives set up far from the house near the marsh. The bees traveled Edge Lea collecting pollen from Ava's delphinium, from her small dwarfed apple tree, wanderers who always returned to this tall man hidden behind a mask. She'd remembered the way his head had bobbed below her waist, the way the hair on his crown caught the light. She watched him grow old, and infirm, with a sense of vindication and despair.

Ava had been bad, perhaps, but that time with Roy had been enough to sustain her for a lifetime. Until the bones had been revealed, pale and small in the dark earth, she had never thought she'd needed more than that. Her baby had been too early, small, and silent. Perhaps she had not lived, and they had spared Ava the truth. Perhaps she had lived only briefly, and they had done what they had to do out of necessity. She would not think anymore about the bones. She concentrated on Diana's baby, who roared out of the womb and wailed, whose limbs cycled and whose eyes met hers with the most daring of looks. "Naughty girl," Ava whispered, and despite the uncertain happiness, the possible misery of the world that awaited her, she placed her in Diana's arms.

Homing

Jules was living in the Maple Farm house with the Mayock brothers, Neil and Philly, when someone from her old neighborhood was arrested for exposing himself to the deaf girl. Neil and Philly had just gotten in from work, and they were sitting around the scarred table with their boots off, wearing gray wool hunting socks. It was winter, so they'd been plowing the Connecticut General Insurance parking lots all night, and Neil had described how the eyes of displaced deer and coyote, peering from the patches of woods left standing on the insurance company's grounds, had sparkled in the truck's headlights. In the middle of the table stood the near-empty bottle of what they'd been drinking to pass the time and keep warm, some of it poured now into their coffees. Outside, the snow continued to fall, blow in under the kitchen door, and drift up along the house's peeling wood siding, covering brambles that Jules knew were lilacs. Mandy was the one who told the deaf girl story, overheard at her parents' doughnut shop counter, where the local men had coffee and smoked and read the Sunday paper. She was swallowed up in Philly's red-and-black-checked coat and a long scarf, which she unwound while she talked, her small hands brittle-looking at the end of the sleeves.

"The guy must be crazy," Neil said.

"Taking it out in this weather," Philly said.

Neil and Philly looked nothing alike. Mandy liked Philly. Jules pretended to like Neil so everything would be even. She slept in his room with him, and she followed through the motions of being his girlfriend, which meant letting him do what he wanted with her and acting as if she liked it. Really, he wasn't her type—lean and lanky and too sweet-natured to be attractive to her. When he stood up his body seemed to unfold. In the pocket of his Woolworth shirt he carried a photo of his dead sister, Laura Rose. Every so often he would pull it out and look at her, and his face appeared to fog over and become unreadable. Sometimes he would say, "Let's ask Laura Rose," and his brother would become solemn, and the photo would come out. They'd sit for a moment, as if waiting for the image to respond.

Laura Rose had died before either of the boys was born. In the photograph, she was a teenager with long, heavy hair that draped her narrow shoulders. She wore a blue peasant blouse, and stood in front of the abundant lilacs holding one of the homing pigeons from the loft that sat empty now in the backyard. For a thirteen-year-old, her eyes were dark and portentous. She held the bird in hands that revealed, to Jules, more emotion than her face—the long fingers of one curved under its breast, the other grasping the tail feathers, cradling the bird's body in a clasp of complete love. After she died, the brothers said, their parents had let the birds go. But they would not live in the wild, and for a long time they returned, fluttering around the closed loft, pecking for seed. It must have been wearying, Jules supposed, to have released them in an attempt to forget, and to never be allowed to do so. Jules had always been afraid to ask what happened to Laura Rose. She assumed it was an accident, or cancer, something that could easily strike any of them, and she felt it would be unlucky to bring it up. Mandy agreed. Neither of them breached what Jules called "the sacristy of Laura Rose."

Now the wind came at the windows, and the old maples scraped the roof shingles. Mandy sat down at the table with them. "Bet there wasn't much to expose," Philly said, winking at his brother. His hair was dark and thick, like Laura Rose's. When he didn't shave, he looked dangerous, almost ruthless, but when he did his face was soft and pale, like the undersides of Jules's arms. Then, she could easily see him in khakis and a sport coat, his feet shod in leather shoes, traipsing the threadbare Oriental rugs at her parents' country club.

"You guys are drunk," Mandy said. "And it's only nine o'clock."

Neil leaned forward and put his elbows on the table. He looked at Jules and raised his eyebrows. "So, you know this guy?" he asked her. When Neil spoke to Jules his voice always altered, became soft and tender, almost *crooning*, she'd said once to Mandy, and Mandy had given her a look as if to say—be *happy*, already.

They had all seen the *Deaf Child* sign in Jules's neighborhood, stuck in the middle of a long strip of tall hedges as if the child lurked there, just beyond the green border. Jules had met Philly and Neil at John Brown's restaurant bar in the town center, and they'd driven her home nearly every night last summer before she'd decided to leave for good and no one stopped her. She knew they imagined the deaf girl's hedge covered with snow, and the girl herself accosted somewhere behind it, the man's pants shucked down around his knees.

"His name is Nestor McAdams," Mandy said.

"I don't know any molester named Nestor," Jules said.

Philly and Neil's mouths opened wide with laughter. Neil slapped the tabletop with his hand, and seemed in pain. Philly laughed at his brother laughing. Mandy flattened her small mouth in the semblance of a smile. She hated it when they drank too much and Jules encouraged them.

"She didn't hear him coming," Philly said.

The deaf child, back when Jules knew her, had been fifteen years old, a babysitter. She had hearing aids and could read lips, and her name was Mary Beth. She twirled the jump rope for

Jules, one end tied to the garage door handle. She made popcorn and brought her own cheddar salt. Foolishly, Jules had told the brothers a story about Mary Beth that fueled their imaginations, and regardless of anything Jules said after—that she was flat-chested and had blond frizzy hair held back with a plastic headband—Philly and Neil invented their own composites, as if they had seen her one day beyond the tall hedge sunbathing, wearing nothing but a bikini bottom. They brought her up at bonfire parties at the reservoir, at the Sound View Pavilion, at the Candlelight restaurant lounge listening to the bad top-forty band. When Mandy or Jules balked at doing something distasteful or unlawful—sneaking into someone's backyard on High Hill and swimming naked in their pool, having sex with the brothers in the same room—Philly or Neil would say, "Let's ask the deaf girl, then." The deaf girl had lived with them all summer, as uncanny a presence as Laura Rose.

"That story can't be right," Jules said now. "She isn't a *girl* anymore."

This quieted the brothers. Jules heard only the scrape of their chairs.

"You always think too much," Philly said. He gave her a long look, one similar to others she had lately struggled to understand. *I love you*, the look seemed to say. Jules didn't dare let herself imagine he meant anything by these glances. She cherished them, believing they were all she would ever have.

Then Neil protested that she needed to exercise her intelligence to pass the high school equivalency exam, and asked her what she'd finished reading. And Mandy said she'd gotten doughnuts for nothing, because no one was eating them, and went into the kitchen. When the looks had first started happening, Jules worried that Mandy would notice. But Mandy expected other things from Philly—things that Jules believed were far too easy to falsify. She wanted him to let her spend the night with him and have sex, and take her places in his car. For Mandy, that was what love meant. Jules had never believed differently, until the first time Philly gave her that look, and she saw in it the possibility of anguish and fear, and she knew that she and Mandy had been wrong.

Now Philly looked away, focused on something outside the window. He leaned forward in his chair. "Damn," he said. "One of the Holsteins is out."

Maple Farm was once a prosperous dairy. Philly and Neil's parents had sold the farm and the adjoining land long ago, but kept the house, where they'd lived and then, later, died. Much of the pasture was sold to developers who built Ridgewood, a community of Colonial and split-level houses connected by a labyrinth of streets named after trees: Maple Hill, Chestnut Edge, Butternut, and Hickory Lane where Jules used to live. The rest went to a wealthy man who cultivated corn and kept a small herd of Holsteins. He had intended to produce ice cream and sell it in a shop, but so far nothing like that had ever occurred. Instead, a few hired men worked the farm, and though the functioning of the business had nothing to do with either of them, the brothers still felt an inherent responsibility toward the place.

Neil leaned over to peer past Philly. "No, that's a black trash bag," he said.

Jules rose and went to the window. The maple trees that grew by the house also lined the narrow road that led to the barn in back. There, through the blown snow and the bare trunks, she saw a cow. The animal struggled through a drift that swallowed her legs. She thought she saw panic in her soft brown eyes. "Oh," she cried. She moved to the kitchen to grab her coat and boots, but Philly was there first.

"What do you think you're going to do?" he asked her. He shrugged on his coat. He grabbed an old halter that hung beside the door.

She had no idea what to do. She had never been close to the cows, only seen them from the yard at a distance, lumbering and lowing shapes whose hooves made small ruts in the spring earth, whose defecated piles smelled up the house and brought large flies that eventually perished on strips Philly hung in every room. She followed him out the door anyway, trudging in his footsteps through the snow. The cold was sharp on her face. She'd forgotten her hat, and the wind whipped her hair around. She found gloves in her coat pocket, and she put them on.

Neil and Mandy had stayed inside, watching from the dining room window. Jules decided that Neil must be the drunker of the two brothers to believe that he couldn't be of any help. She followed Philly back toward the red barn where the cow stood, making a snorting through her large nostrils. Just beyond the cow the woods began, private land marked off by barbed wire that the new owner had sold, but that the cow knew, and had treaded through each spring and summer on narrow paths to the pond and fresh clover. The cow made a frightened lurch deeper into the bank. Jules stayed a bit behind.

"Good girl," Philly said. "You stay there."

Jules thought he was talking to the cow, but he had turned to look at her over his shoulder, his movements slowed, his voice low. The wind blew through the bare trees, clanking the branches. Then he told her "Shhh," and she watched his two hands rest on the cow's black-and-white flank. She could not, for the wind, make out what he said, but she heard the low murmuring of his voice, its soothing cadence. She saw his hands move, flat-palmed across the cow's back, and she was reminded of Laura Rose's hands in the photograph, their grace. He had the halter around the cow's neck in moments, and tugged gently to lead her out of the drift and onto the path back to the barn. Jules stepped away. She turned and saw one lone shape in the dining room window. She gave it a little wave.

The sound of the gun's report seemed, later, as lost in the wind and the snow as Philly's voice calming the cow. It had an echoing quality, as if from a great distance. Hunters, Jules thought, then wondered how far the ring of trees extended before Ridgewood. Out of the corner of her eye she caught sight of something scampering back under the barbed wire and into the woods, a long tail flying behind it like a dog. She turned once again toward the house and saw Neil, standing in the road between the maples, drop the family Remington as if he had just taken aim. Behind Jules, Philly lay in the snow—splatters of red like petals strewn around his leg. He was grunting, and breathing through his nose, as the cow had been moments before. She knelt down in the snow beside Philly. She found his hand in the snow and she held it to her face. His eyes were closed and she told him to open them.

"Open them now," she said. And he did. There was the look again. She held his hand to her mouth. Philly pulled her down into the snow with him so that their faces touched, then both their mouths, warm and desperate. The snow was in her hair, packed into the sleeves of her coat, melting around the neck of her sweater. Jules heard the cow low. She felt the warmth of Philly's mouth. And then Neil was there, the snow spraying up around his heaving body as he scrambled through the drift. He didn't say anything. He took the halter off the cow and tied a tourniquet on Philly's leg. It was only his leg, after all. While he tied, Neil cried openly, and Jules felt an awkward sorrow for him. Philly swore and remained conscious. The bloody leg steamed from its snowy spot. Mandy called an ambulance. Neil carried Philly into the house and left a trail in the snow, and another trail across the kitchen linoleum. Mandy handed Philly the bottle from the table with a shaking hand. Once inside the house, Jules felt her heart step up, as if it had been held dormant for the time she'd been outside holding Philly's hand to her lips. She did not let herself think about what else had happened. It seemed that under the circumstances no one would mention it, and so she would never have to. Neil sat down, shaking and cold.

"It was a coyote," he said. He covered his face with his hands.

Philly told him he always had terrible aim. He told him everything would be fine. Jules kept her arms by her sides, her coat still on. She could not believe him.

Later, after they took Philly to the hospital, Mandy went around with a damp towel, cleaning up the blood, and Jules said she would go out to find the cow. She stood by the bloody spot in the snow, and remembered the way Philly's mouth felt. She saw that the cow had followed the path to the barn, and stood now by the barn door, where she had found some protection from the wind. The snow had dwindled to flurries that melted on Jules's face. It was afternoon, but the sky was gray, and it could have been any time of day. Jules supposed the barn was locked, but she tried the latch, and it opened and the cow went in past the others that stood munching straw or swishing their tails idly. She thought that the animal might know where to go herself, and it was enough that she was inside where there was food and other cow bodies for warmth, and no threat of predators. The barn smelled of hay and feed corn and the cows themselves, a heady scent, almost sweet. Jules found she liked the sound of their movement—the placing of their hooves, their snorting and swishings.

When she was a child she'd visited Auer Farms, a 4-H farm, on a field trip with her first-grade class. They had all worn their uniforms, plaid skirts, and white socks, and she remembered her shoes had gotten sucked into some mud on the trail, her socks had been splotched, and she'd been mortified. She'd begun to cry, and the other girls had thought she'd wet her pants or thrown up, and they took her to the teacher, who smelled reassuringly of J'Adore and patted her head and told her, "Not much longer," as if the trip itself was disdainful. And it had been—smelly and dirty, and the men who worked there, from a distance, seemed tired and overheated, wiping their faces with the backs of their hands.

Now, she breathed in the smell of the barn, and remembered Philly leading the cow, the gentle way he urged her, the shape of his hand on her flank, then the blood in the snow, and his mouth, its suffering, the pieces of bone and skin and shredded jeans, all of this—her revulsion and horror, her need and her desire, fastened together, a confused blending. Jules felt it would be wrong for her to stay in the house with the brothers any longer, so she went inside to pack her things. Mandy watched her from the doorway, holding the bloody towel. She didn't ask what Jules was doing. She stood there, the towel bunched in her hand, fingers bloodstained, face swollen from crying.

"What if they have to—you know?" she asked Jules.

Jules had her duffle bag on the bed. It was the bag she'd taken to Adventure Camp two summers ago, when she'd gone to Costa Rica, snorkeled and hiked and done everything the brochure promised with teens of her own age group. She had come back from the trip with no clearer idea of how to fit into her own life, and a liking for Camel cigarettes, and a knowledge of the varieties of expensive pot.

"What are you talking about?" Jules asked. "If they have to, they have to."

Mandy was Jules's first friend out of high school. Mandy graduated last spring, a year before Jules would have if she'd stayed. She worked now at the doughnut shop and made enough money to buy Philly a leather jacket for Christmas, and Jules an antique gold locket she'd seen at a shop in Simsbury. Mandy said that she was following the *no-plan* plan, that one day she would simply choose one of the boys in town, get married in the Sacred Heart Church, and begin having children, much as her own mother had. Now she stood glaring at Jules.

"What are *you* talking about?" she said.

"Philly's leg," Jules said. "Aren't we both talking about Philly's leg?"

She continued to sort through the pine bureau, separating her things from Neil's and placing them into the duffle bag. Everything smelled of the pine drawer. Jules knew that when she got wherever she was going and unpacked, this smell would remind her of the house, of Neil and Philly, and then, in a heart-wrenching way, of everything else.

"And you think that's okay?" Mandy said. Her voice had risen to a high pitch. Jules looked at her and wondered if she was having an emotional breakdown. When her mother had one, this was the first marker: a kind of high, whining tone to her voice, a thrashing of her arms and whatever she was holding at the time—frozen peas, the blow dryer, a pair of high-heeled pumps. Soon, the items would resist the thrashing and once freed, sail across the room. Jules glanced at the towel in Mandy's hand. As Mandy became more agitated, Jules's movements slowed, like Philly with the cow.

"I think," she said, carefully, "that Philly will still be himself, with or without a leg."

Mandy's eyes widened. "Are you kidding me?" she said. The towel flapped at her side. Her voice rose again. "You're not *leaving*?"

Jules stopped packing. She knew Mandy was crying, and it was just like her mother, the exasperation and disbelief, the begging for Jules not to go, and then Jules staying for a while longer, a feeble attempt to make everything work out peacefully. Part of her knew she had never wanted to leave then, or now. Part of her longed to stay, to be condemned to the torture of imagining Philly and Mandy in bed each night in the room across the hall, to wait in silence for Philly's glances, to suffer Neil's attention.

"Neil will think you blame him," Mandy said.

Jules had not thought about this—how it would look to abandon Neil just then.

"And what about me?" Mandy said.

Jules glanced up at Mandy's face—the mascara streaks, the reddened, upturned nose, the sprinkling of freckles. She sighed and unpacked her bag. She had only put in her summer things, anyway. She didn't have anywhere else to go.

After a few weeks, Philly came home without his leg. At first he could not climb the stairs, and like his father when he had gotten too old, he settled into the back room. It was set up as a kind of den, with wood-paneled walls, a fold-out sofa, and antique duck decoys on the shelves. There was a television, and a phone extension—a whole little world. The room was at the back of the house, with a view of the old loft, and the sun came up in its windows and shone across the fields. Philly lay there, ashen at first, and then as the days passed, ruddier and stronger, and hobbling around, content with the prospect of his prosthetic limb, and walking just as Neil, or the Malucchi brothers, or Lew Vancour, or any of the other town men did. Jules spent each day in the living room chair by the window. She had a set of the Harvard Classics, green leather books with gilt pages that Neil picked up for her at a tag sale. She didn't want to tell him that the books probably wouldn't prepare her for the exam. She accepted them, as she accepted everything from him, because it made him happy. She read Aristotle and Marlowe and Plutarch. She read *The Tempest*, the same lines over again, distracted now by Philly's presence. Though they were often in the house alone, he kept his distance, and Jules understood this as his way.

Mandy worked more often—the night shift when the doughnuts were prepared fresh for the morning. When she came in she smelled of sugar and fryer grease. She slept alone in the upstairs room. She covered her revulsion as best she could. Philly seemed not to care. "It hurts him when I weigh down one side of the mattress," Mandy said. No one really believed her, a woman who weighed only ninety-five pounds, but everyone pretended to understand. There was a bit of an investigation into the accident, with the police coming out to ask questions as a formality. Later, there were rumors that Neil had shot Philly out of a jealous rage. Rumors, Jules saw, grew out of threads of truth. She saw, too, that the multitude of possible truths made almost every story impossible to believe. She wondered if Neil had told someone what he'd seen between Jules and Philly in the snow that day, if he'd known what he'd seen, if he'd even seen anything. All of this kept her awake at night, staring at the plaster ceiling, avoiding Neil's arms and legs thrown out in sleep.

She had begun cleaning the house, exploring the rooms and finding left-behind things that she read as clues to something she needed to know, its origins placed in the bloody snow by Philly's lost leg. Laura Rose's old figure skating trophies packed in newspaper. Bits of sequins on a closet floor. Pads of notepaper with lists in old ink: *string cranberries, salt front walk, call Maureen.* Grocery items she found remarkably personal: *Ban roll-on, bobby pins, Corn Flakes.* And then the notebook and its contents, observations and lists written in a girl's rounded script: *Luna, Sophia, Mystic, Ariel,* and beside *Ariel,* the penciled word *Lost.* There were notes describing markings, *noble, white-breasted,* and Jules understood that these were Laura Rose's birds.

She lay in bed beside Neil and thought that here his mother gave birth to three children. She imagined the wet sheets wrung in her hands, the blood, the window tossed open and the cooing of pigeons, the blazing maples, their leaves shivering and damp with dew. Or the scent of lilacs, and the bees in the farmhouse eaves, the maple shadows moving on the lawn each evening. Long ago, there would be a lighting of candles, and the lowing of the cows, the crickets rimming the old stone foundation. Jules felt Philly waiting in the room below. She felt his even breathing through the floorboards, heard him turn, and the sofa bed's springs recoil. Soon, when the snow had melted, the fields would lighten with mayflowers, and Jules saw there was a window of time in which he might come to her, and still, he did not.

She began sleeping on the couch in the living room. The living room was cold and drafty, and the couch's cushions were flattened and uncomfortable. Jules awoke each morning before the others, and folded up her blankets and put them away. Still Neil did not protest. His face took on a drawn, pensive expression. By March, everyone was sleeping in a different place in the house, and the snow had melted in the sunny, high fields, and the cows stepped cautiously across the half-frozen ground. Philly was walking with a cane. One day he came out of the den and found Jules folding up her blanket. He raised his eyebrows at her, but said nothing. He had stopped giving her his old glances, as if the kissing in the snow had been all he needed from her. She wanted to ask him why he was up so early, but she did not. She wanted to know why he did not wish to talk to her, or look at her, but she kept quiet. The silence in the house was something no one seemed to want to breach. They simply looked at each other, and moved away in opposite directions—Philly with the tapping of his cane, Jules with her arms full of the blanket.

She took the blanket to the closet under the stairs. There she had found a Hush Puppies shoebox filled with eyedroppers, and Ace bandages, and a small bottle of dried Mercurochrome. She imagined Philly and Neil's mother dressing their small cuts when they were boys. Across the hall was Philly's den, the door open, and the sun coming up through the windows onto the rumpled sofa bed. She went into the room to make the bed, believing Philly had gone. She liked being in the place where he'd slept, to smell him on the sheets and the quilt. She pulled everything straight. Out the window, two pigeons perched on the loft's buckling roof. *Sophia, Eileen*, she thought. Laura Rose's father would drive the birds in crates and release them. Each time, a little farther distance. These locations were marked in her book—*Granby, Southwick, MA*. Her notes recorded the weather—*gray, breezy, rain*. The times each returned; the birds that didn't. Jules pictured her waiting under the maples in one of the old porch wicker chairs, winding her long hair around her fingers, watching the summer sky. She turned now and Philly was there, a presence in the doorway. He smelled of the outdoors. He still wore his coat. Jules felt herself redden, as if she'd been caught.

"The pigeons," she said.

Philly leaned over to see out the window. He stood and smiled, amused. "Ghost birds," he said.

"But you see them," Jules insisted.

She looked out again at the loft. The birds were gone. She did not know why she'd mentioned them at all. This was why no one spoke, she decided. They never said what they wanted. The words were shields to hide behind. She reached for his coat and opened it, pressed herself against him. Philly wrapped his coat and his arms around her. She had her ear to his chest, and heard his breathing. She was conscious of not wanting to unbalance him. She heard him groan, and she remembered the day in the snow, and thought of his pain. When she tried to pull away he whispered not to. His mouth was in her hair, his hands on her breasts, sliding below the bones of her hips. When he kissed her it was different than the time in the snow. It was gentle and probing, like a question. She would answer with her body on the sofa bed, the door softly shut, the sun awash on the quiet duck decoys.

They were not discovered, and in the days afterward, Philly acted as if nothing had happened. For Jules, it was enough that it had. From this she imagined a moment when Philly would announce his feelings for her. A time, perhaps, when Mandy would begin to come by less, and then, after a while, notice someone else at the doughnut shop counter—a boy with a cap over his eyes, a sly smile, and a car with shiny rims in the parking lot. Though it had been Neil who asked Jules to live in the house with them, and Mandy, initially, who introduced her to the brothers, the prospect of being with Philly made Jules happy, assuaging her guilt. Nothing appeared different, but beneath her silence was a churning she could not contain. She was cheerful, and slept later on the couch, heedless of discovery. She asked about pigeon feed and talked of resurrecting the old loft. There had been pigeons the other day, she said. Mandy gave her a worried look. Neil became grave and reproving.

"There haven't been birds for years," he said.

Philly stood in the doorway and said nothing.

One Sunday morning Jules caught Philly coming down the

stairs from his old room. She felt light-headed, watching him descend. Mandy came down a while later, her expression vacant, her freckles bright. It was as if, sensing what Jules wanted, Mandy had changed her mind. It may have been that it was spring, with everything pushing to the surface—grass blades, tree leaves, crocuses and daffodils whose long, slender stems emerged from the loamy soil, tender and exposed. The lilacs budded and opened and bobbed on their branches. That afternoon, the four of them sat around the living room watching a *Bonanza* marathon. The television picture was unclear, the images separating particles. They had been drinking White Russians that Mandy had mixed up in the kitchen with milk that Jules thought might be sour. It was April, almost Jules's birthday. She would turn eighteen, something that once seemed pivotal but now did not. Outside, rain pelted the maples' new leaves, and it was dim and shadowy in the house.

"I hate this," Mandy said. "Little Joe never gets the girl."

"He gets a lot of action," Neil said.

"But nothing long term," Mandy insisted.

"Only Little Joe wants long term," Philly said.

Neil groaned. "Jesus, Philly," he said. "Don't speak for everyone."

Philly had his prosthetic leg off, and Mandy sat beside him, something she usually refused to do if he didn't wear the limb. "Why, Neil," he said. "Are you thinking *long term?*"

Neil shrugged. He looked ridiculous, holding the white drink. Jules felt sick and had stopped drinking hers. She looked beyond the violet glare of the television to the couch, and saw Mandy's hand snake up the back of Philly's shirt. Jules had seen her do this before. She would draw a picture on his back with her finger and ask him what he thought it was—a flower, a sun, the letters of her name. After a while, Mandy reached over Philly and grabbed his prosthesis, where it lay beside the couch. She held it with two hands in her lap and stroked it absently, while on the television Hoss balanced his large body on his galloping horse. The grass was trampled and dust sent up. Shots rang out, and Little Joe cried miserably for his dead fiancée.

Mandy stood up with Philly's leg in her arms and stepped away from the television glare into the shadow. Jules saw that she was crying, too. Philly looked at her, incredulous. Neil glanced up and seemed to shrink back into the chair cushions.

"What is wrong with you?" Philly asked.

"I'm holding your leg," Mandy said. She held the prosthesis out and gave it a shake. The joints made a sound like a marionette. "Isn't anyone sad about this?"

For some reason, the brothers both turned to Jules. At first, she thought they blamed her, but then she saw they simply expected her to quiet Mandy down. Jules stood up from the couch and took the limb from Mandy's arms. Mandy was unprepared, the leg slipping easily into Jules's hands. It was soft textured plastic. Lightweight. Jules had held it before, that other morning in the den. She held Philly's leg now and did not know what to say, overcome with love. The brothers' eyes shifted from Mandy to Jules. Mandy's mouth opened a little in surprise. Her cheeks were still wet with tears, but her eyes narrowed.

"Oh, you were sad all right," she said. "You were packing to leave that day until I stopped you." And then Mandy's face darkened, sensing her betrayal, and she grabbed the leg back. Philly kept his gaze averted, pretending to watch the television. On the farthest couch, Neil bowed his head, his hands in his lap.

Jules saw her mistake unfurl and bloom, a taste in her mouth like the soured milk. It was true that Philly loved her. He had done so at the moment he believed he might die, and later, when she'd gone to him willingly, her love her own wound. Yet as long as Neil cared for her, Philly would never admit it. She had left herself open to his advances, his violations, believing they ensured her a place in his life, in this house. But that, too, had been an error. Neither of the brothers thought much about the house, or their mother's labor in the upstairs bed, or the way their dead family's hands had worn down the banister. If she had shown them the lists in their mother's handwriting, the Camay soap packages saved for a sweepstakes, their father's notes in *The Old Farmer's Almanac*, they would have shrugged and shaken their heads. If they noticed the bats flying from the attic on summer nights, they never mentioned them. The pigeons that returned, forced by their terrible yearning for home, pecked at the grass and found nothing.

Jules sat back down on the couch, quiet, dulled by these thoughts. The story she'd told the brothers about the deaf girl had been made up. Once, when Mary Beth was over babysitting, a boy had stopped by. Mary Beth had let him in, and they'd sat together watching a movie with Jules. After, Jules had been sent to bed, but she'd lain awake for a long time, wondering about the boy and Mary Beth, and what they might be doing together. She'd slipped downstairs to the room with the television, its sound soft, a lull of music and intermittent voices. The room, like this one, was dim, filled with particles of light. She told the brothers that she caught them both without clothes on her mother's couch—Mary Beth's body pale against the dark upholstery, her long hair draped down the cushions to the floor, and the boy on top, Mary Beth's hands clasping his buttocks, smooth and childlike between her bent knees. Really, Jules had found them sitting much the same way as she'd left them. Maybe they'd been holding hands.

Jules remembered Mary Beth, the times she'd looked at Jules with a sad, loving glance when she'd done something she shouldn't have—torn her mother's evening gown playing dress up, taken her father's Princeton class ring and hidden it in her own ceramic jewelry box. The way she'd smooth Jules's hair with a gentle hand, a girl assured of what was right. One who would always know when she should have what she wanted. Jules had hidden for a long time behind the loveseat, watching Mary Beth and the boy, but nothing had ever happened, and she'd gone back to bed. As a child, she hadn't known what she was waiting to see. Later, the few times she herself had babysat and had boys over, she'd been the one naked on a neighbor's couch, her own legs spread, fervent for something that would be, time and again, evasive and heartless.

Jules saw the rain outside on the maple leaves, against the old glass panes. She saw Mandy's hand slip back under Philly's shirt, and Philly's mouth moving, which meant words were coming out. *Tree, house, window.* But they could be any words, or words that meant nothing. Jules knew she would do one of two things. She would go to Neil and take his hand in hers, lean in to press her mouth to his, requesting forgiveness. Or she would pack her bag and leave. Someone would surely pass her walking with the heavy duffle, see the way her hair hung in lank strands against her wet clothes. A car would stop for her—a Plymouth with finned lights and dark upholstery, and a smell coming out like peppermint and cigarettes. Behind her, up the road in the house, Neil would pull out the photo of Laura Rose. Jules's story floated in the room, waiting to be told.

The Philter

I met Sarah Brinker in the old DeNitto's Grocery & Drugs on a day of spring thaw. The melted snow dripped from the store's ravaged awning. She was perusing the narrow aisles of light bulbs and canned hams, herring and boxed matches. She wore a beautiful camel coat, and the dark scarf of her hair fell over the coat's shoulders. When I was a child, my mother, too harried with the four of us to put on her makeup, would order her groceries, the glass bottles of paregoric, over the phone, and DeNitto himself in his white coat would deliver them in cardboard boxes to our Cape on Cider Road. Sarah Brinker wandered up and down the aisles, and I watched her from the newspaper stand where DeNitto's son had placed free coffee—Styrofoam cups and little packets of sugar, milk beginning to sour in a small chipped pitcher. She interested me, a tall girl, a teenager making her circuit past me. The man who worked the register would have let her wander the aisles all day, so I went up to her and asked her if she was looking for anything in particular. I had the time to be bothered.

She stopped and looked at me, her eyes pale green, her nose mottled with freckles. "I just like the smell in here," she said. Then she smiled, soft and too sad-looking for a girl her age.

DeNitto's did have a particular smell—like fennel and sage, like camphor and licorice, a smell filled with the complicated history of the place, first as a meat market with sawdust on the floor, a drugstore known for opium tinctures and hand-rolled pills, a five-and-dime filled with cheap toys. Outside the door, propped open to let in the spring air, the awnings dripped onto the sidewalk, and the cars rushed through the intersection on their way to the winding roads and cul-de-sacs of nearby neighborhoods. The outside air only heightened the smell of the store, and I smiled back at her, remembering days when I'd come here with my friends to slip packs of gum into our pockets, and old Mr. DeNitto would glare at us from behind the register, never suspicious enough to accuse us—good girls from families of early town settlers, founders of the Carriage Club, whose membership excluded him.

Sarah turned then, as if to move away from me, but hesitated and turned back.

"You could do me a favor," she said. Her voice, low, conspiratorial, forced me to move in closer, and I smelled her coat, and the scent that came off her hair, not altogether clean. She asked me to buy her tampons. I must have seemed surprised, because she went on to explain that she had the money, but that her mother had always purchased them for her, and her mother had died, and she was too embarrassed to buy them herself. I felt sorry for her then, and I agreed, and she pointed out the ones she wanted, and handed me a little roll of bills that I had to unroll at the register—a fifty, a twenty, and three ones, all wound up tightly together. I found her waiting outside, her eyes brightening as I came through the door.

"Thank you, thank you!" she said, taking the bag.

"I'm Kit," I told her. I put out my hand and she took it solemnly.

"So nice to meet you," she said. "I'm Sarah. You saved me. That guy at the register is weird. I didn't like how he looked at me."

People, she said, often looked at her strangely. Her mother used to tell her it was because she was *striking*, but Sarah said that it was her sister the model who received the admiring glances.

"They look at me like I have no arms," she said. "Or three eyes."

We walked along the sidewalk, past Hilliard's chocolates and the children's shoe store. She told me I seemed like a kindred soul, and that was why she'd asked me to make the purchase for her. "I knew when I saw you," she said. "I could see that we were fated to be friends."

I began to correct her, to tell her I was too old to be a friend, but then I wondered how that would sound, and what it would make me if we weren't friends, and I didn't like the idea of telling a girl whose mother had died, who might very well need friends, that I wasn't one of them. I asked her where she went to school, and what subjects she liked best. And she said she'd been out of school since her mother died, but before that she'd excelled in all of her classes.

"I'm afraid I wouldn't do well in them now," she said. "They send the books and the work home, but I'm too bored to do it."

Bored, a word that didn't quite fit. Then she took a package of cupcakes out of her coat pocket, tore the cellophane, and held one out to me. We'd reached the corner, and I saw my car parked in the public lot behind the shops. I looked at the cupcake, and then at Sarah, at her pale face framed by that dark hair, at her pleading eyes. I should have gotten into my car, driven home. There are things you do that you later learn to regret, that flummox you, unimaginable things that make you pause and reconsider who you really are, what you are capable of. These things you spend a lifetime pretending you've forgotten. The stolen cupcake was rich, filled with sugary cream. When she asked me for a ride, I told myself I could not refuse a motherless girl.

Sarah lived on a narrow lane in a new subdivision lined with trees behind which houses sat as if along a ridge, their muted colors blending into the landscape. The houses were made of timber and fieldstone, slate roofs and walls of glass that caught the sun and flashed heliographic messages through the wooded front yards.

"That's it," she said. I slowed at the house and made to turn in the driveway, but she grabbed my arm. "No, don't. Keep going."

"Why?" I asked. I glanced up the drive and saw a powder-blue Mercedes convertible parked near the garage. "Is there something wrong?"

Sarah had settled back in her seat. "Just drive up the road," she said. "I'll tell you where to go next."

"Sarah," I said. I must have sighed. I saw my good deed taken advantage of, Sarah directing me to some boy's house where a group of teenagers skipping school played the stereo and mixed their parents' alcohol.

She looked at me, and bit her lip. "I'm keeping you from something," she said. "I'm so sorry. I just thought you had the day free like I did."

To me, *free* meant *empty*, a large space waiting to be filled, hours like cylinders lined up in some vast machine. I'd stopped sleeping by then. My husband had left town on business a week ago. He'd invited me along, but I'd declined.

"You're going to have an affair while I'm gone," he'd said.

He was sliding his belt into the loops of his pants. We'd just had sex, an unspoken requirement before he left. I'd looked up at him from the bed as if he was someone I didn't know, which is what he'd begun to seem. My mother had told me to be leery of men who accused me of infidelity. She'd had a girlfriend in high school who'd married just this kind of man and suffered the consequences. "I don't want to call your house and find the phone out of order," my mother had said. "I don't want to be the one to find you shot dead in your sleep."

I watched my husband tightening his tie. "Well, you're wrong," I said.

I'd already had an affair that ended badly, one he knew nothing about. Since it ended I found myself adding a shot of whiskey to my morning coffee, drinking it while I sat by the front window watching the squirrels dart beneath the shrubbery. I'd add it to my iced tea at lunch, and then while ironing, or emptying the dishwasher, the drink would come with me, from room to room as I cleaned, and sorted, and chopped vegetables, while I waited for my husband to return from work. I was trying to stop, which meant filling up my days with something else, avoiding our house and the cabinet with its assorted bottles, the rooms where the air seemed removed, like the roped-off rooms in museums—Mark Twain's house fashioned after a steamboat, dim with melancholy; William Gillette's castle bedroom, his velvet dressing gown draped at the foot of the bed; Harriet Beecher Stowe's parlor filled with gilt-framed art, her doily-covered breakfront—places I'd visited trying to fill my days. I'd reached the point where I'd consider driving this girl around all afternoon, being whoever she wanted me to be. But I knew that I shouldn't let her know this, that I should allow her to convince me first.

"If you explain to me where you'd like to go, and why you don't want to go home, I might be able to help you," I said.

Sarah shifted in the passenger seat. She flipped down the sun visor and looked at herself in the mirror.

"I like being in your car," she said. "I like riding around. When I was a baby my mother used to drive me around the neighborhood in the car seat to make me stop crying."

She flipped the visor up and turned to face me. We'd reached the end of the street, and the stop sign, a place where the trees met overhead, the branches bright with green shoots. "Turn left," Sarah said, and I did.

She directed me through a labyrinth of narrow roads, the houses all tucked away behind stone walls, the trees growing tight along the sides. All the time she chatted about her collection of antique Limoges demitasse cups, how her grandmother started her with her first set, a rare pattern from the 1800s.

"My sister and I would go to her house," Sarah said. "She'd have a little white iron table set up and we'd have a pretend tea party with cookies, and Coke instead of tea in the little cups."

I came to another stop sign, and she leaned forward as if considering the route. "Turn left," she said.

"Again?" I said. I told her it felt like we were making one large circle.

"You're smart," she said. "Pull over here."

There was a stretch of woods, and just enough room on the shoulder for my car. Sarah climbed out, crossed the road, and started up through the trees. I could make out the shape of her coat. "Come along," she called. "Giddyup."

I got out of the car. The wind blew cold, the weak sun slipped low, and I breathed in the scent of the woods, the wet trunks, the fern beginning to uncurl, the violets blooming on their delicate stalks. The woods leveled off at a meadow where Sarah stood waiting for me to join her.

"Brinker's Field," she said. "Site of model airplane launches. The Super Buccaneer took off here and made a loop the loop in 1982."

She was a little out of breath, her cheeks rosy like a child's. She set off across the field, and I followed, silently, waiting for some explanation. Our shoes sank into the mud. Sarah laughed at me when I complained. I noticed how pretty she was when she laughed, her pale green eyes a strange underwater color. We reached the edge of the field and a scattering of glacial rocks where the woods began again, and we climbed up on one, its surface sun-warmed and smooth. From this vantage point the woods dropped away, and below us I could see what I came to understand was Sarah Brinker's house. It was late afternoon, the sun dipping below the tree line. The lights in the house were on and the windows revealed the interior—an open space with long, white couches and a large canvas on one wall that from this distance seemed to be a painted blot of sunlight. We sat on the rock and watched the people moving about inside—first a gray-haired man in a cardigan sweater who emptied a cup into the sink, then a young woman, older than Sarah, heavier, slower-moving, climbing an open staircase, turning on a lamp in an upstairs bedroom. The woman faced the window and pulled her shirt over her head, the movement fluid, as if choreographed. She walked to the closet in her bra, and then she reached behind and unhooked that and let it drop to the floor. She undressed entirely and went through the bureau drawers, her skin very white in the lamplight. A shadow of a figure came to the bedroom door, and you could see the woman's shoulders deflate, the way she turned her head away as she spoke, all of this revealing her annoyance. I noticed the arm of his cardigan sweater, and I knew it was the gray-haired man there, just beyond the door frame.

"She's getting fat," Sarah said quietly.

"It's not nice to spy," I said. I didn't want to sound prescriptive, like a parent, but I didn't know how else to rein in what had begun to feel uncomfortable and wrong.

Sarah sat with her knees pulled up to her chest. "Is that what we're doing?"

Of course she included me in this. I'd followed her through the woods and the field. I sat beside her on the rock, staring down into the lighted house at the naked woman sorting through bureau drawers, at the shadow of the man in the doorway.

"Do you come here a lot?" I said.

Sarah shivered and pulled her coat sleeves down over her hands. "Only when I want to see what's really happening."

Then she pushed herself off the rock and stood there among the old fallen leaves, the saplings' lithe trunks rising up behind her like dancers. "Let's go," she said.

I hesitated. I could return to my car, leave this place, and forget all about Sarah Brinker, but she seemed to have read my expression.

"Do you think you should leave me alone with them?" she said.

I looked past her to the lit-up bedroom, to the woman spread out now on the bed, her legs draped over the edge, and the man in the doorway. I felt strange, light-headed. My hands shook.

"Who is she?" I asked. I imagined it was the father's new young girlfriend, or the housekeeper, or a nanny hired to monitor Sarah's comings and goings. Sarah's face became very still. The sun turned the sky, the tips of the new leaves on the trees, a pinkish orange. The woods smelled of black birch and snow. Below us on the lawn, crows pecked at the dead grass, their feathers dark and oily, bodies huddled together amid the covered patio furniture.

"It's my sister," she said. Then she turned and started down through the woods and the crows scattered, cawing a warning cry, lining themselves up in the tree branches.

I followed her down through the woods, past a garden enclosed with a picket fence, around the side of the house to the front door. Here the evening seemed to have descended quicker, and the automatic lights lit up as we walked along the narrow slate path. I whispered for Sarah to stop, to wait, and she turned to me before she opened the door. I didn't have time to protest. She had the door open, and her icy hand gripping mine, pulling me into the house, into the smell of something cooking—a dense, heady scent of herbs and meat, the cooking steaming up the big windows. I felt dizzy with hunger and longing.

"Hello?" Sarah called out.

To the left the open staircase led up, and beyond it the living area spread out with its spare, white furnishings, the painting like an opening of brightness on the wall. I looked out the windows into the woods, and imagined them green and waving in summer. Sarah kicked her muddy shoes off in the entry, and I stood there in mine, trying to scrape some of the mud off on the mat. It was a few minutes before the gray-haired man came down. His tread was silent. He wore moccasin slippers. "It's you," he said, smiling. He looked at me then and the smile never faltered.

"Hello there," he said.

"This is Mrs. Joan Cully," Sarah told him. She looked at me as she said it, her eyes filled with mischief. "My science teacher from school."

The man's eyes lit up then. "Wonderful! A disciple of *De rerum natura*. You'll join us for dinner." He extended his hand and I shook it, thinking I should correct all of this, that as the adult I was obligated to set him straight. *Your daughter is a liar*, I'd have to say. *She's making this up.* But I'd come so far, and I couldn't see any way to extricate myself.

"This is my father, Dr. George Brinker," Sarah said, almost primly. "Or Georgie, as we call him."

"So nice to meet you, Dr. Brinker," I said.

"Just call me Georgie," he said. "Come, I'll get you a drink."

The promise of the drink was enough to lure me into the living room, to take the proffered seat on the long white couch, to accept the tumbler filled with ice and gin and a slice of lime. "It's spring," Georgie said. "I thought we'd have a tonic."

He sat down beside me and put his feet up on the coffee table—a heavy wooden slab with a carved base that I imagined might have once held the feet of some European baron. He cradled his drink on his chest. "You're familiar with Lucretius?"

Sarah sat in one of the chairs across from me, twirling her long hair, watching us. "St. Jerome says Lucretius Caros was driven mad by a love philter," she said. She grabbed her hair in her hands in imitation of the madman.

Georgie sipped his drink and eyed her. His face reddened. "You know better than that." He looked at me and shook his head in commiseration. "Young people want to believe the most fabulous stories."

I smiled, sipped my drink, and waited for the woman upstairs to descend, but she did not. Georgie began a lecture on Lucretius and his contribution to Epicurean physics, and I imagined he must be a classics scholar, and all that was needed was a refreshing of his drink and a prod by Sarah to launch him onto a new topic. In this way my presence was simply as audience. At one point Sarah wandered from the room and came back with a cracker, which she nibbled, pretending to listen. Georgie's voice seemed to reverberate near the vaulted ceiling. Every so often he paused and looked to me for affirmation, which I gave with whatever I felt fit—a smile, a laugh, a shake of my head. I found I wanted to please him, that I was both leery and enamored of him—his chiseled chin, his eyes a shade darker than Sarah's, his gray hair clipped close to his head, almost pelt-like. When he spoke he moved one hand in the air, and I admired his long fingers, his trimmed nails. I couldn't banish the memory of him lurking in the upstairs room, the woman's bare legs dangling from the bed, and this image darkened the edges of the man I sat beside, made him even more desirable.

A timer went off in the kitchen, but Georgie and Sarah both ignored it, and the woman came down the stairs wearing a silk robe, her feet bare. She padded across the wood floor to the kitchen and proceeded to take the roast out of the oven, set plates and casseroles on a table that looked like a barn door on trestles. She lit candles. Then she stepped into the living area, in front of the now darkened windows.

"It's ready," she said. Her face was very beautiful, but blank, as if the life had been siphoned out of it. Her robe had slipped, and one bare breast was almost entirely exposed. We all stood, Georgie and me with our drinks, both of us a little unsteady. He took my arm and leaned into me and said something in Latin, and I smelled his cologne, felt the brush of his cashmere sleeve.

"This is my daughter, Miranda," Georgie said.

The woman looked me up and down. I saw her notice the mud on my shoes, but I didn't care. Georgie explained who I was, and Miranda narrowed her gaze.

"You must be new," she said. "I don't remember you. I had Mr. Neubaum for science." She spoke in a slow, even voice. She brushed her hair over her shoulder. "Is he still there?"

Sarah stepped beside me. "Do you want to sit by me or Georgie?"

And Georgie took my arm and his hand slid down to my hand

and I felt its softness. He tugged me to a place at the head of the table. "By both of us," he said.

I watched Miranda take her seat, noncommittally, and spoon food onto her plate, and eat, her eyes on the food which she cut up first into small, even squares. I tried not to think about Sarah's dead mother, or the scene I'd witnessed from the hill above the house. I couldn't make sense of it, and yet I felt what I'd seen made the room tense and charged. Georgie ate in silence. At one point he set his fork and knife on the plate and finished off his drink.

"We were talking about Lucretius," he said to Miranda.

I could see she didn't want to look up from her food, but she did, slowly, and nodded. "That's nice," she said, and I heard the bitterness in her voice. "The nature and mortality of the soul."

The drinks had taken care of my sense of taste, and the food was just something I lifted on the fork to my mouth. The silence settled, squat and solid, a block of ice that made the room cold at our backs.

"So, Sarah tells me you're a model," I said.

Miranda's mouth flattened. Sarah moved the food around on her plate. I heard her fork scraping away at the porcelain.

"Some years ago Miranda won a national teen modeling contest," Georgie said. "She was signed to Eileen Ford."

"Now she works at the mall," Sarah said.

"Miranda's returned to the university," Georgie said. "She's studying literature."

"She used to live in France," Sarah said.

Throughout this exchange Miranda stayed quiet, her head pivoting between her father and Sarah, the food forgotten on her plate. The candlelight did a dipping sort of dance. I heard a far-off sound of a car door slamming. Miranda cocked her head, listening.

"Sounds like Mummy's here," Miranda said.

"Oh, shut up," Sarah said.

Georgie rose quickly from his seat. "Girls," he said, his voice anguished.

He looked to me as if for help in managing them, and I realized he thought that as a teacher I should have this skill. I glanced at Sarah, whose eyes had welled, and then at Miranda, whose face had suddenly become filled with a lovely light.

"I'm so sorry about your mother," I said to them both.

Miranda stared at me. "What do you mean?"

I turned to Sarah, questioning, confused, but she focused on her plate, the fork suddenly stilled. I expected her dead mother to walk through the front door, set her purchases from Saks on the floor, and apologize for being late to dinner. Georgie's face paled.

"Oh, Sarah," he said. He shook his head. "I apologize, Joan. Drama is our Sarah's forte."

Sarah glared at her father. "Oh, Georgie," she said. "Don't pretend you don't know where she is. I'm going to take a spade out to the garden. I think Mummy's roses need their roots aerated."

Miranda put both her hands down flat on the table and pushed herself up. She began to clear the plates, stacking them carefully, gathering the silverware. Georgie reached blindly for his drink.

"I think I saw some crows out there this afternoon, pecking at the soil. Pecking and pecking," Sarah said. She leaned toward her father, her face stony. "This morning there was a dog all muddy from digging."

Miranda held the plates in her arms and moved toward the kitchen. I heard the clatter as she dropped them into the sink, and then a sob. Georgie made a silent exit in his moccasins, and Sarah and I were left alone with the guttering candles, with the cold coming off the dark glass.

"I'm going to leave," I told her. I stood and pushed my chair back. The house itself felt alive and vibrating, and I imagined that anything could happen here, that anything might have already happened. We could hear Georgie speaking quietly to Miranda.

"You can't go," Sarah hissed. "Don't you hear them in there? Conspiring? Don't you believe me?"

She rose and came around the table and took my hand and held it to her cheek. "You're all I have."

I yanked my hand away. It struck me then how foolish I'd been. Hadn't I done the same thing, said the same words to the man with whom I'd been sleeping? In the dark little guest room at the back of his house I'd pressed my face to his chest and begged him to believe in my love for him. Sometimes we become so good at slipping into a dream that we convince ourselves we can make others fall into it as well. If we just show them our versions of the world, they will relent. Outside the guest room a tree bough had clawed at the window. The room was cold, and little used, the bed narrow and covered with a damp comforter. Upstairs, his house held his children's rooms, the dining room where he carved the roast, the den where he put his feet up in his recliner and read his golf magazines, the evening paper, the book he claimed he'd begun, about which we'd made our first connection. He lit fires and his children gathered round in nightgowns and little footed sleepers. In the kitchen his wife prepared meals from recipes in a cookbook propped open on an ornate stand. On days he and I met I could smell the spices she'd used the night before—cardamom, ginger, rosemary—the scent of them trapped in the comforter's folds. Once he'd asked me why I didn't want children, and I remember being surprised he'd assumed that the absence of children in my life meant I didn't want them. I had rooms in my house waiting for children, I wanted to say. But I did not. I let him believe what he needed to believe about me. I let him imagine me, just as I had imagined him.

Sarah stared at me, grief-stricken. And then before I could move toward the door Georgie and Miranda returned—Miranda with her blank expression, carrying a tray of cups and saucers, Georgie proffering a cake on a crystal platter.

"Oh, no, Joan, please," Georgie said. "You must have dessert."

He set the cake down on the table, and came over to pull out my chair. "It's been complicated with their mother gone," he said. "The girls each perceive the situation differently."

Miranda cut the cake, one glazed with fruit and giving off a cloying, almost perfumed scent. She served the coffee while Georgie poured the brandy. I sat quietly, accepting the cake, the drink in its crystal snifter. I didn't know if Sarah and Miranda's mother was dead, or if she'd run off with a lover. I didn't wonder why Sarah believed she was buried in the garden. Any of these things could be true, and the possibility of them filled the night with something clandestine. I felt the power of their secret, and I wanted to know it. Sarah stared at me across the table like an unrequited lover. Her cake sat untouched on its plate.

"We all process absence in our own way," Georgie said. "Don't you agree?"

I nodded, carefully. After the man had ended our affair, I'd driven daily past his house, waiting until the hour he returned from work, letting him see me passing as he fumbled in the driveway with his briefcase, his house keys, forcing him to call me. "Please stop," he'd said. "It's no good what you're doing." He told me to give it time, and soon it would seem as if it had never happened. How could I tell him that was what I'd feared most? I leaned toward Georgie and touched his hand.

"I understand," I told him. The words felt heavy, caught on my tongue.

Miranda's eyes fell to our joined hands.

I stood and asked for the restroom, and Georgie stood along with me and said he would show me the way. He led me down a hallway, the glass on one side reflecting our passage, the wall on the other a burnished paneling. He opened a door and I followed him into what appeared to be, in the dimness, the master bedroom. He flipped the switch in the bathroom, and a swath of light cut across the wood floor. "Here," he said. We stood in the darkness together a moment. My head swam. I sensed him standing near me. I heard him breathe. I remember thinking that if he reached for me I would let him take me into his arms, but he did not. He stepped out of the room, closing the door behind him.

The bathroom was made spacious by mirrors in which I glimpsed my blotchy face, my windblown hair. In a Victorian novel I'd be described as "blowsy." I laughed at myself, at the word. I came out into the dark bedroom and felt along the wall for the door I believed would lead to the hallway. Instead, I found myself in a long closet. On either side of me I felt clothing—dresses made of crepe de Chine, nubby herringbone sleeves, soft gabardine, all infused with Chanel No. 5. I smelled the shoes lined up on the floor, the scent of leather and sweat. I imagined Sarah's mother standing here, damp from her shower, choosing her outfit. I wondered what her name might be, and then I understood with a clutching feeling that I knew her name—Margaret Brinker. I'd read about her going missing months ago in the newspaper, how she'd met foul play, the tragic outcome of a home invasion. There had been a rash of burglaries at the time—the targeting of homes during the hours when the occupants were at work and school. The man I'd been sleeping with had joked about them choosing his house and discovering us. "What a surprise they'd have," he'd said, dipping his head, working his mouth down the length of me. But that was what the authorities surmised the woman, Margaret Brinker, had done—come home in the middle of the day and encountered them.

I reached out and touched a sleeve of a blouse. I ran my hands through the clothing, pressed my face into a fur. Once, while the man I'd been sleeping with had dozed I'd slipped upstairs, found the room where he'd slept with his wife, and gone through his bureau drawers, his closet. I found his neck ties hung all together, a dizzying swirl of colors and patterns. I'd looked at the woman's things as well, sorted through her jewelry and taken a pair of earrings—small pearls, innocuous, impossible to miss. Later, he'd accused me of taking them, and I'd denied it, feigning shock. "You must have been targeted by the burglars," I'd said. But after that I'd been disheartened that he would think me capable of such a theft. The earrings had ceased to hold any mystery once he'd suspected me of having them. I left Sarah's mother's closet without taking anything. I found the bedroom door and followed the hallway back to the open room where Georgie bent over the fireplace, balling up newspaper, feeding it to the flames. Miranda loaded plates into the dishwasher. I tried to remember more of the newspaper article, what had been written about the woman: housewife, member of the Junior Women's Club, the meager evidence—a shoe, an empty purse, blood. *Margie and Georgie*, I thought.

Sarah sat beside her father, watching the kindling catch. She glanced at me when I entered, but that light that her eyes had once shown me was gone. Georgie stood and Sarah stood alongside him.

"She isn't really my teacher," she said.

Georgie looked, not to me, but to Sarah. "Now, Sarah, don't start."

"I just met her at DeNitto's," she said. "I don't even know her."

She smiled then, a little sadly, as if to say, "Forgive me, but you've been no help at all."

Georgie made his protests but I waved them away. I was still Mrs. Joan Cully, science teacher. "It's late," I said. "I should get going."

I heard him behind me voicing his concerns, his apologies. I fiddled with the latch on the locked door, turning it the wrong way before he reached past me to open it. The night air held a sharpness that surprised me. It rushed into the house, filled with the smell of damp soil. I imagined the roses' bright shoots, budding lilacs clambering over fences. Georgie stood with me on the slate walk.

"You'll need this," he said, enveloping me with his cashmere sleeves, slipping the sweater over my shoulders.

His face bent to mine, and I thought he intended to kiss me and I pushed him away. His face registered shock, a look of dismay. He held his hands in front of him to signal his innocence.

Behind him I saw Sarah, her long hair, her bright eyes. I called
to her over his shoulder. "I'll see you in class." I couldn't remember why I had come. Georgie stood in the lighted doorway as I
walked along the slate path. The shoe had been here, I remembered, on the path. A woman's pump, filled with blood. And
then more blood, at the entry, the purse thrown there, in the
rhododendron. I kept to the path and reached the driveway, but
when I heard the hollow echo of the front door closing I slipped
around to the back of the house. The woods extended up, a tangle
of brambles and twigs. I would have to cross Brinker's Field but I
could imagine the way I'd come—I had no doubt I could find my
way back. Inside the house Sarah might have been encouraging
Georgie to put in a call to her headmistress to verify her story. I
imagined them coming after me, and I felt urged to hurry, to put
distance between us. Georgie's sweater snagged on a briar and I
yanked it free. I slipped once, then twice, losing ground on the
incline, grasping in the dark for saplings to stop my fall. Around
me the woods pressed like the folds of clothing in Sarah's mother's closet. I pushed on, my feet sliding on damp leaves. I heard
my harsh, panicked breathing. When I reached the top and the
rock where Sarah and I had sat, I felt the burgeoning relief that
comes with a narrow escape—a thudding clap of joy. I looked
down and saw the house lit, torch-like and golden, and the sisters
standing in front of the window looking out. My movements, like
a small, furtive animal, had been masked by darkness, and yet I
knew Sarah looked to the place she believed I had gone. Miranda
lifted one hand to her sister's shoulder. In the halo of light from
the house I saw their mother's small garden.

I crossed the field under the moon. There was no one to see
me. I thought I might lie down in the muddy grass and rest. Then
I considered the small animals making tracks over me in the
night, nibbling the spilled food on my blouse, and I moved on. I
came out of the woods on the road at the wrong place, but I could
see my car, and I reached it, easily, and got inside. I'd left the keys

in the glove box, and I got them out and started the car up. Of
course I was turned around, directionless. The road loomed dark
and empty, narrow and winding, the trees arched overhead like
a bower. I drove for a long time. I thought I might follow the
road forever, winding one way then the other, trapped in some
enchanted maze. I understood Lucretius, crazed with love, a heat
without a source. I wanted to drive past the man's house and in
the cover of darkness step up to the windows of his den and peer
inside. I needed to see the happy tableau—wife, children, father
with his feet in socks. If I could look at him one more time I
might remember the anticipation of his mouth, his hands, the
smell along his collarbone, the smarting feeling of his bristled
chin. The trees scraped the side of my car, a noise like a ratchet,
and then I heard another sound—a heavy, hollow thud. A trash
can, a mailbox, a deer taking a hesitant step onto the asphalt.

Even now I am unsure about the events of that night. Whatever
evidence existed to tie me to the Brinkers and their neighborhood has been erased—my fender repaired by a mechanic in a
town miles away, a small shop along the Connecticut River where
my father once took his Chevy Corvair; DeNitto's and its stock
of opium potions burned to the ground, the son a suspect in an
insurance scam. I don't ask myself if the retired judge, having
fallen asleep watching television and awakening to remember
he'd forgotten to retrieve the mail, stepped into my headlights
on Deer Run Drive, or those of some other driver. Was the earth
in the garden freshly turned? Did Sarah Brinker choose me in
DeNitto's, or was it the other way around? I hit something, my
heart swift and winging in my chest. I left it behind me, and I
drove on.

An Heiress Walks Into a Bar

Esme told him that when she was twelve, three things happened of notable significance: her grandfather presented her with a car, and then died in it; her grandmother had a pool installed in her basement; and her father put on his pale blue pinstripe suit, custom-made for a previous trip to the Bahamas, and left, never to be heard from again. These events meant something, finally, as Dean motored her out among the Thimble Islands. It was April, a day with the unfulfilled promise to be warm. The wind did its own kind of dance with the Sound. Dean wore a straw hat anchored under his chin with rawhide, his hair in a ponytail, and shorts. Esme avoided looking at his knees exposed to the chill. He piloted the boat between the rocks, quiet and purposeful. She almost loved him for his disinterest.

An hour ago they'd sat in the seafood restaurant lounge on Main Street, the only patrons at eleven a.m. The place was dim, the chair she sat in damp and sticky with the sloshed liquor of uncountable drunken mishaps. The light came through the front window and made her feel dissolute and pale, like someone who might, according to her grandmother, have *crawled out of the gutter.* She wore her mother's pearl earrings and a too-small T-shirt that her grandfather bought for her in a gift shop in Rio de Janeiro the fall before he died. She'd found it in a drawer in the upstairs bedroom of her grandmother's house, a shirt she'd worn and abandoned years ago as a teenager. She'd left the house early that morning and stopped at the bank. In her bag was enough cash to create a stir, to provide five times the yearly salary of the bartender, a girl whose sharp wrist bones made her seem fragile and terrible all at once. Esme could barely look at her lifting the bottle of J&B.

Dean slid his drink alongside hers and pulled up a stool, and offered her his hand. When she mentioned his ruddy cheeks, he said that there was a lot of wind on the water.

"Oh, do you live on one of the Thimbles?" she asked him. He shook his head no and stared at her.

"What are you looking at?" she said. She was drinking the whiskey with ice, and had asked the bartender, Patsy, to add a few maraschino cherries. The TV was on—a news channel showing a white car being pulled from a river.

"Are you married?" he asked her. He bit his lip, waiting for her answer. His eyes were the color of slate. Esme hated to disappoint him if he was trying to pick her up.

"Officially," Esme said. "My marriage is in a state of limbo."

She thought she might divorce her husband, Douglas. She'd driven the day before from Boston and the house where they lived with their three-year-old son to her grandmother's house in Connecticut. Douglas had already tracked her down on the phone.

"What do you think you're doing?" he'd asked her. Esme imagined him saying, *young lady*, like a chastising parent. Behind him she could hear the muffled anguish of the hospital's waxed floors, fluorescent lights, and life-support machinery. She heard him paged on the intercom.

"I want to see my Nana," Esme said. "Why make it out to be something it isn't?"

"I know what this isn't," Douglas said, suspicious.

Esme was a little surprised that he'd guessed. "This is nothing," she said. She began to laugh, something she could never help doing when she was caught. Even as a child playing tag on the front lawn. Later, in lies with boyfriends. Douglas grew grave over the phone and said something about little Dougie, left behind with the nanny, and she hung up on him.

Dean set his drink on his white napkin. Patsy swiped her towel near them, the undersides of her wrists like the musculature of a dissected bird.

"Good enough," Dean said to Esme's admission of a dissolving marriage.

"For what?" she asked him, winking, a little ashamed.

Esme's grandmother had left her grandfather years before he died, and she lived on dividends from stocks in one of the suburban neighborhoods built from the dissolving of the old Connecticut dairies, on pasture land and orchards and pine woods. Once, cows tread stony paths across her front lawn, through the place that was her living room. Her house was a 1950s Colonial, with aluminum siding, and shutters, and bay windows. Alice was an avid swimmer. As a young woman she'd swum in amateur competitions around the country, and aspired to qualify for the 1936 Olympics. She had trophies and photographs that Esme saw each summer at the Thimble Island house—her favorite was of Nana in a white bathing cap, thin and long-limbed, diving from the island's granite outcrop with the house behind her. She swam in the Sound when the weather was warm enough, or in her backyard pool, but in the winters she missed her exercise, the buoyancy, the light and youthful feeling of moving through water. When Esme's grandfather died, her grandmother received a small inheritance, and with this she commissioned a local company to install an above-ground pool in her basement. She had to call all of them in the phone book before one would comply. She had to pay extra for them to do it.

The pool was a model called the Astura, the sides fashioned of redwood like a barrel, eighteen feet in diameter and fifty-two inches deep. The effect of the pool on coming down the basement stairs was one Esme would not forget. The ceiling flickered and shimmered. The smell of chlorine mixed with mildew. Her grandmother decorated the basement—strung old postcards from Hawaii and the Bahamas on a wire, draped faded leis and the hollowed-out halves of coconuts. People gave her plaques with sayings: *The Ole Swimming Hole, Swim at Your Own Risk*, and a vintage one made of tin, *The Plunge, Admission, 10 cents*, that showed a bathing beauty and her boyfriend poolside, the woman dangling her feet into the water. There was a lamp on a telephone table, but also an overhead bulb at the base of the stairs, and a strand of small paper lanterns. The pool pump hummed. Children were not allowed to swim in the basement pool. Esme could only sit on the gritty stairs and look down while her grandmother swam in a circle around it, her arms long and thin, her gray hair tucked under her cap. Esme sucked on a toffee, stolen from the silver dish in the dining room. Later, her grandmother's bathing suit would hang over the upstairs shower rod—a paisley print, paled by chlorine.

In her nineties now, Esme's grandmother spent afternoons watching soap operas and smoking cigarettes with her live-in caretaker, Caridad, whom Esme paid to stay with her. At four o'clock they had aperitifs. Recently, her grandmother had given up the basement pool—the stairs, the ladder in and out, were too hard to maneuver. Esme told Caridad to let her grandmother do whatever else she wanted. They listened to piano sonatas on the record player, the recordings scratchy, the tones of the instrument eerily magnified, its hollow sadness entering all of the rooms. Yesterday, Esme had visited a doctor and been given a startling diagnosis. The man was a respected colleague of her husband's, someone she could not doubt. Everything following this disclosure seemed different, overly vibrant: the path leading to her car littered with apple blossoms, like torn confetti, the sky filled with birds and their sharp little song. Like her mother, her own ovaries, once small almonds nestled in her pelvis, were under siege. The doctor had discussed stages, and plans of action. Esme had gone home and packed a bag and fled. When she arrived at her grandmother's, the lawn was painfully bright and green, and the dogwood blooming showy, and she was aware that these things used to please her, and now all of that had been lost. Caridad met her at the door.

"Who is it?" her grandmother called out from the depths of the house. "Who *is* it?"

Caridad called back in Spanish.

"For the love of God," Esme heard her grandmother say. "Say something I can understand."

Esme saw her come into the room, holding onto the back of a chair, then a loveseat, moving among the furniture for support. She had grown portly. The tops of her feet in her flats looked bruised. Her hair, all white now, wasn't done. Usually, Caridad got her dressed for company, but Esme hadn't let her know she was coming. Her grandmother paused by the bureau with the lamp. She looked at Esme in the doorway. She didn't have her glasses.

"Well?" she said. "You're letting in the Japanese beetles."

She didn't know who Esme was. "It's me, Nana," Esme said.

Caridad had on a pretty skirt and low-heeled pumps. Her hair was dark and curly and she wore familiar emerald earrings. She smelled of Esme's grandmother's Chanel.

"Look, Alice. It's Esme."

Esme's grandmother wore her old swimming robe that snapped up the front. She hadn't acknowledged Esme at all, but instead had groped along the top of the bureau for her cigarette box and gotten one out. She stood with it in her fingers.

"It's not time for a smoke," Caridad said. "So you can forget about the light."

Esme thought her grandmother might curse Caridad. Instead, she threw the cigarette at her. Esme went up to Alice and put her arms around her. The old swimming robe smelled of the moth-balls they'd scattered in the basement to ward off chipmunks.

"How are you, Nana?" she said.

"Why are you here?" Alice asked. "Where's your mother?"

When her grandmother had begun asking this question, Esme would feel lightheaded, as if some terrible mistake had been made, and her mother was still alive and she was responsible for her whereabouts. But then she had grown used to saying the words. *My mother is dead.* Her grandmother always ignored her. Today, she seemed to think Esme's mother was at the shore. This set her talking about the Thimble Island house.

"I hope she knows to bring enough kerosene," she said. She moved over to a chair. The sun came in through the sheers and patterned the carpet near her feet. "She needs to tell the Grandisons I won't be coming this summer."

Caridad told Esme she would make her lunch. "I have just what you want, *querida*," she said. Then she disappeared through the butler door into the kitchen, and Esme sank into the couch's down cushions. She put her head back and sighed. The sun fluttered around her grandmother's bony, crossed ankles. Her skin was the color of uncooked pastry.

"Light my cigarette," her grandmother said. "And I'll tell you a story."

Esme closed her eyes. "Not now," she said. She let the sun move across her eyelids. She smelled the new grass through the open window. She pictured her mother at the Thimble Island house, sweeping sand, turning the broom to get between the floorboards. The sea air blew through, heavy with salt and the smell of the seaweed caught up on the rocks, drying in the sun. Her mother swept. Her father's footsteps sounded above them. There was the opening of old drawers, and then his footsteps descending, and his pause, a shadow in the doorway. Her mother continued with the broom, ignoring him. Esme watched her sweep and cry, sweep and cry. This was the time her mother had awoken her father in the middle of the night and told him she needed a doctor. Her father had put them all on the dinghy and they'd motored in, a treacherous ride, her mother doubled over, her arms folded and pressed to her stomach. They'd waited in the hospital emergency room for word, her father clutching Esme's hand. The doctor came out and told him her mother had lost the child.

"What child?" her father had said. He'd let go of Esme's hand.

She was five then. She remembered it all now—the white glare of the small hospital waiting room, the vinyl cushioned seats. She'd been in her nightgown, and it was wet at the hem. She saw again the dark look in her father's eyes, the eyebrows drawn together. He had been handsome, tall and heavily built, a football player in college. That night he'd sat hunched and small. He rubbed his hand over his eyes, over and over, as if he might wipe away something disagreeable. The doctor had cleared his throat, and walked off in the wake of his mistake.

Esme remembered the terror of the nighttime dinghy ride, and her mother later washing the sheets, the blood on them turning the water a rusty color. They had been cream-colored, patterned with summer flowers. She had been afraid of sleeping on similar sheets after that, always seeing the splotches of dried blood among the phlox and nasturtium and iris.

In the kitchen, Caridad sang a song in Spanish. Esme heard her heels on the linoleum.

"What is all that noise?" her grandmother said. "Who is in the kitchen?"

Sitting on her grandmother's couch, Esme ate the sandwich Caridad brought her on one of her grandmother's china plates.

"This is the Wedgewood," her grandmother said, drawing on the trustworthy details of the past. "Your grandfather gave me this set the first time I caught him having an affair."

"Oh, Nana," Esme said. The bread was soft and white and stuck to her teeth.

"I have eight sets of fine china," she said. She held the long cigarette in her hand. Occasionally, she brought it to her lips and inhaled, and then realized it was unlit. On the tip was the imprint of her lipstick. "It was what he bought me when we fought. Not flowers or candy. China."

Dean—surprise, surprise—was a songwriter. His hair was a fine red, held back in its ponytail with an elastic band decorated with pink polka dots.

"Is that your daughter's?" Esme asked him, pointing, chewing her ice.

He gave her that flustered, frustrated look she'd grown used to from men. "I don't have any children," he said. He shook his head, his hands out. He'd been in the middle of telling her about his band. Now, he turned away with his drink.

"Aren't you going to ask me if I have children?" Esme said.

"No," he said, annoyed.

She told him her plan had been to have lunch at the Pine Orchard Yacht and Country Club. Her grandmother was still a member.

"Those were her explicit instructions," Esme said. "I was to order clams casino."

Dean glanced over his shoulder at her, his eyes slit, doubting her. "Let's head on over," he said. "We'll hit the links after."

Esme smiled, unsure. "So you like golf?" Dean gave her another look, and hunkered down over his drink. He had a habit of spinning his red plastic stirrer around and around in his ice. Patsy kept replacing the napkins beneath his glass. When she did she'd glance up into his face, briefly, intimately, as if she were relaying a secret message.

"We played last night at the Puppet House Theater," he said.

Esme remembered the theater and the shows there. The puppets were rare, made by an Italian craftsman. They stood five feet tall—knights and peasants and kings in robes and armor, their faces hand-carved wood painted with fiercely distinct facial expressions. They fought with swords and killed each other, lopping off heads. Esme told him the puppets frightened her as a child. She didn't say that her father loved them and the medieval stories they acted out.

"It was a perverse fear," she said. "Every summer I begged to go see them."

Dean said he'd forgotten the place was once a real puppet theater. The performances had stopped long ago, and he'd never had the chance to see one.

"What's the name of your band?" Esme asked him.

Dean finished his drink. "Godspeed Nelly," he said, sounding pleased.

She reached across the bar and took his hand in hers and pushed up his shirtsleeve. On his forearm was a tattoo of a mermaid. "You look like someone who enjoys an adventure," she said.

He smiled at her with his silly wet lips. "That depends."

Patsy stopped her noisy stacking of the bar glasses, watching.

"Do you have a boat?" Esme asked him.

Often, when she was a child summering on the island, her father would motor her about in the dinghy. They would go inland to pick up something that Esme had usually wanted on a whim. Strawberries for shortcake. Watermelon candy. More Nancy Drews, because she had finished the ones she brought too soon. Then, they'd go to the Blackstone Library, and she'd check out all the ones she hadn't read. Her father would stop, sometimes, at one or two of the islands on the way back. Cocktails at Cut-in-Two, or Potato Island, with a friend. Esme sat on the rocks, reading, the pages dampened by the sea. She'd have the mystery solved by the third chapter, or she'd have the story better than the one that Carolyn Chute ended up telling. Nancy would kiss Ned. They'd make out in the moss-covered mansion, in a room quieted by cobwebs. Esme would stare out at the sun setting, kick the brown snails off the rocks into the green water. She was a good *waiter*, her father told her. He'd nearly upset the dinghy getting back in.

Esme paid the bar tab, fumbling with the thick stack of bills. Dean looked at her, and looked away. She slid off her stool and he followed her out of the bar. They stood in the sunlight and blinked at each other. His boat, he claimed, was at the Pine Orchard dock. He didn't have a car, so Esme drove the two miles to the country club. Dean sat stiffly in the Mercedes, and in the light Esme saw that his khaki shorts were grubby. His wide-brimmed hat hid his expression. She pulled into the dock's gravel lot and parked. The dock was quiet. His boat turned out to be the yacht club launch, a long antique wooden craft with oars and benches with life vests tucked underneath.

"This is yours?" she said.

"In a manner of speaking," he told her. He helped her into the boat and explained that as a teenager he had run the launch as a summer job. "There you go, pretty lady," he said, like a southern gentleman. The wind was different from how she remembered it—harsh and cold. The sea flipped up little taillike waves. They slipped between the moored sailboats, the small islands of bedrock, stealthy and sleek in their stolen boat. Her father had told her the stories of these islands. They'd been named by the Mattabeseck.

"*Kuttomquosh*," she said. Dean looked at her from under the brim of his hat. He smiled, nice even white teeth. "Beautiful sea rocks," she said. In this place a man once took off in a hot air balloon. A tiny circus performer fell in love and left initials in a rock. A pirate was rumored to have left his gold. There were crevices and hidden places, tide pools plundered by cormorants, paths overrun by poison ivy, diving boards anchored into the granite, cottages on stilts connected one to the other by wooden footbridges.

Esme remembered the dinghy dipping, and her father singing

on the way back, *Will you go, lassie, go? And we'll all go together,*
the song her grandfather sang when he brought the car on her
birthday, an emerald-green Austin-Healey. One of her grandfather's neighbors had it in his garage and wanted to sell it, and he
thought of her eyes when he saw it. He'd driven the car to her
house himself against the wishes of his team of doctors, who'd
ordered him, after his bypass surgery, to recuperate longer, to
take it easy and read or take walks in the fields that were his
property—*woman's activities,* he'd said, a little disgusted. Standing
there beside the car in the driveway, he'd sung her a bit of a song
with a fake, lilting, Irish accent, the words of which she'd tried
for years after to remember—*Oh the summertime is coming and
the trees are sweetly bloomin'.*

Esme's mother had come to the doorway of her studio and
stood with her hand on her hip. "What's going on out there?" Her
voice held that suspicious tone she used when she tried to assume
some authority about things that should have, but didn't really,
matter to her. *How many cupcakes did you eat? How late did you
stay up last night? Did you do your Latin homework?*

The car sat shining on the black tar drive. Esme's grandfather
did a kind of jig around it. Esme felt anxious about the incision
in his chest. He'd shown it to her in the hospital, peeling away
the loose covering to reveal the sutures, harsh and sore, and she'd
turned white enough for the nurse, who came squeaking back
across the linoleum threshold, to wonder what was wrong with
her and offer her a chair, and place a palm to her forehead.

Esme had thought her grandfather's skin looked like the flesh
of a plucked turkey, the kind her father got at the game farm for
Thanksgiving, that sat on the counter in the kitchen, the flesh
gaping where he stuffed it. Her grandfather wore a suede coat,
and one of his lambswool sweaters, and a shirt under that, and
maybe even an undershirt, the scar held safe beneath the layers
of clothing. He was thin, and his slacks bagged against his legs.
The snow had melted from the driveway, and the lawn showed

wet and yellow and muddy in patches. The river water moved in the distance with the sun on it—a pearly black. It had been a mild winter. Esme had been reading E. E. Cummings and thought every day seemed like *just-spring*. Her grandfather sang, *And the wild mountain thyme grows around the bloomin' heather*, or something like that. *Will you go, lassie, go?* Her father was at work, assuming more authority at her grandfather's old New England rubber company. Her mother had been painting in her studio, a cottage-like structure covered in dead vines, the gnarled wood wet and black against the siding. The studio sat separate from the main house, under a stand of ash at the end of a pebbled walkway. Her grandfather told Esme to get in behind the wheel.

"What are you doing?" her mother called out, her voice a little higher pitched now. She stepped out of the doorway.

Her grandfather gave her mother a disdainful look. "I want her to sit in it. Get the feel of it."

Esme slipped onto the leather seat. It smelled of her grandfather's cologne, and cigarettes. Esme looked up at him. "You're smoking," she said, softly.

Her grandfather's eyes were merry and black like the river. He sang part of the song for her. He put his finger to his lips.

Esme thought later that she had played a role in his death. Hadn't he brought the car for her? Done the jig? Hadn't she kept his secret about the smoking? He had asked her mother if he could take her for a spin, and she'd said, "No," flatly, unwavering. "No," she said, her voice dull and hard as the frozen ground. Esme's grandfather sighed. He looked at Esme and winked.

"Slide over," he whispered. He'd moved his chin to the side, a slight movement.

Esme would have done it, quickly, before her mother could stop her, but the stick shift was in the way. Her mother stepped down the pebbled walk, angry now. "I said no, I said it," she called. Her voice was panicky.

"Don't *you* have an attack now," Esme's grandfather said. He

looked at her with concern. Esme's mother came over to the car
and grabbed Esme's arm and pulled her out. Her hands were
splattered with paint—the color turquoise, which clashed with
the car.

"I'm sorry," she said. "The car is lovely, really lovely."

Her grandfather seemed hurt. Esme had wanted to climb back
in. Her mother turned away for a moment, and Esme saw his
face change. A quick switch, from a pained expression, to one of
canniness, and mischief.

"I'll take it back to my house," he said.

"She's twelve," her mother said, softer, nearly pleading. "She's
twelve."

Esme's grandfather got into the car. Esme felt the shaking of
her mother's hand clasping hers. She did not know whom to
protect. She was forgotten for a moment in their exchange, one
of silence and glances she did not know how to read. Her grandfather backed the car up out of the long drive. The sun flashed
weakly on the shining body. On the way home he drove the car
off the road and into a large tree by Mills Pond that crumpled
the hood and flushed out the starlings and wrens and sparrows
gathering colored Easter grass, human hair, dryer lint, bits of
yarn and twigs for nests. Esme was never told if he died from
his heart giving out, or the force of the blow, and she didn't tell
anyone what she knew—that she might have been with him, and
died, too. That if not for her, he might not have ever bought the
car in the first place. This was the mystery that Esme believed,
at the time, was never revealed. Later she would come to learn
there were other things her mother kept quiet.

Dean told her he hoped they were going to dig up some buried
treasure. His voice echoed off the water and the rocks. The motor
whined and churned white. Esme glanced at him, but only out of
the corner of her eye. The cottages were vacant, the islands still.
Dean's bare knees made her squeamish, like her grandmother's
body in her bathing suit—vulnerable veins and creases made by

sagging skin, exposed parts that shouldn't be seen. On the occasion of her grandmother's seventieth birthday, Esme's mother brought crustless tuna and egg sandwiches cut in triangles, a small cake, and champagne down to the basement pool. There were folding chairs set up around a table with a linen cloth. Her grandmother's friends stopped by, some of the same people who had been at her grandfather's funeral. This time, the women wore brightly colored dresses, and the men wore Hawaiian shirts. Esme watched the women's delicately mottled legs descend the stairs, listened to their noises of surprise. Their faces were tan, from Bermuda, or Tortola. Their jewelry, their silver hair, shimmered in the reflection from the pool, in the lantern light. The snow piled up against the basement windows. Upstairs the house was quiet and closed off. Someone, a nephew, had contacted the newspaper, and there was a column written about Esme's grandmother's pool, and her swimming, and they talked about that. Her grandmother, in her dry way, had told the columnist, "Oh, I splash around."

There was a record player, and the music of their voices. Esme went up to the pool's edge and put her hand into the water. She wondered when her father would get there. She asked her mother, twice, how much longer. Her mother, the last time, turned an angry face toward her.

"Stop it," she'd said. She'd given her a glass of champagne. "Don't ask me any more questions."

On her hands was the turquoise paint, small remnants of it under her fingernails. Esme looked at it with horror. She sat at the top of the basement stairs and drank the champagne, which made her cry. She believed her father would find her there, and pity her, and take her home, but he never came to the party. In the weeks after her grandfather's death, Esme's father seemed to fade. She thought now that was only how it seemed. He was setting things right at the company, fitting into his new responsibility. He was out nights, meeting with customers at the Officer's Club. His presence was felt, sometimes, when she arose for school. She'd hear his music early—Melanie, and Gordon Lightfoot. In the bathroom, the smell of his shaving soap. In the kitchen, a glass coated with tomato juice in the sink. Sometimes, the garage door left open. This may have been how it always was. The boat hit a bit of wake—a fishing boat passing out beyond the Thimbles, and she noticed Dean glance at her, watching how she rode it. If she had been tossed in she would have swum the distance.

"I'm a good swimmer," she called to him. "I have my grand-mother's genes."

After Esme's father left, Esme and her mother had driven over to her grandmother's house to tell her. Three weeks had passed, and they hadn't heard from him. He was officially a missing person, but one who had set things in order first—seen to the functions of the company, settled his affairs. It was a gray day, threatening snow. The pools of water from the previous snowfall's melt froze over. Out in the cornfields the broken stalks showed through, brittle and flayed. Esme's mother had spent the weeks without her father baking, and on Esme's winter break from school she joined her. They rose in the morning and left the beds unmade. Her mother brewed coffee, which she drank all day long, the cup clutched in her hand. Her slacks, her sweater, were covered with flour. They'd made pastries, turnovers and cobblers and tortes, and an apple cake that they wrapped up to take to her grandmother. Esme's mother's family, German immi-grants, had once owned a bakery in Philadelphia. Esme's mother had found the old recipes when she cleaned out her father's house after her mother died. They were written out in ink on yellowed paper, folded into a hatbox with a woman's silhouette on the lid. Esme's mother talked, as she baked, about opening a bakery herself with the old recipes. Esme stirred and licked the spoons and watched her mother grow thin. The more she baked, the less, Esme decided, she ate. Each day would bring a new recipe.

"I think today we'll try out these cream puffs," her mother would say.

Everything was a preparation for the new bakery.

"We'll rent that place in town next to the tailor's," she said.

Esme knew of the dusty storefront window. She and her friends would go to the center after school and walk the sidewalks of the outdoor mall. They'd slip into gift shops that smelled of scented candles and steal earrings and small tubes of fruity lip gloss, hiding them in their parka pockets. The empty store used to be Munsen's, a confectioners. She'd gone there with her grandfather to pick out chocolates for her mother. "Which would she like?" he'd ask her, relying entirely on her judgment. His eyes would twinkle. Esme could not choose. His cheek was beside hers—rough, smelling of cologne. The place was hot, and close. The glass case held white doilies covered with chocolates, all the same to her. She didn't say anything about the store when her mother mentioned it. She put the bowls in the sink to fill with soapy water. She cleaned off the spoons. She wondered what might happen next.

Esme's mother hadn't talked about her grandfather after he died, and now she didn't talk about her father. Once, Esme asked her when he was coming back. She'd assumed he left on a business trip. Her mother had said she wasn't sure. She said it as if she believed his returning was inevitable—offhandedly, without concern. Esme wondered then if her parents would get a divorce. She hadn't ever heard them fight, but the house was big enough to conceal any angry tones, to muffle any sharp movements, or thrown objects. Large enough to hide what might have happened. In the afternoons, Esme's mother spent time on the phone, papers spread out on the dining room table, her cigarette smoke spiraling up into the spokes of the chandelier.

At her grandmother's, they climbed out of the car and Esme still smelled the baked fruit and crust on her clothes. Her mother walked ahead of her up the slate walkway to her grandmother's house. Her heels clicked. Esme knew that beneath the camel coat her mother's slacks hung around her hips and bagged in the back.

Her arms were gaunt, the elbows large and pointed under her shirtsleeves. Her hair was dry and colorless on her coat's collar. They stood at the storm door, Esme with the cake, her stomach tight with anxiety, her heart racing with sugar. They rang the bell and waited.

"It's not quite her nap time," her mother said. Esme saw she fidgeted with her pocketbook snap.

They waited, facing their reflections in the storm door. Finally, her grandmother came. She looked at them through the glass, the ends of her hair wet from her afternoon swim. Esme could tell her grandmother was annoyed to see them. Behind her the house was warm, the lamps lit. Esme held the heavy cake, and believed her grandmother might not let them in. But then she did. Once her mother had given her the news, her grandmother lit a cigarette. "Where'd he go?" she asked.

Esme's mother seemed to think she hadn't understood.

"We don't know, Alice," her mother said, calmly, carefully.

Esme's grandmother gave her a knowing look. She had gone into her bedroom and put on her earrings and lipstick. "Just like his father," she said. She exhaled. She looked at her daughter-in-law as if she had just really noticed her.

"Did he take the money?" she said.

Esme thought her mother would cry. She saw her eyes fill, like a child.

"He left it for me," she said. "All of it."

Her grandmother's eyes widened in surprise. "Not like his father," she said quietly. She stubbed out her cigarette.

Outside the living room window Esme could see the pasture across the street, the grass in frozen yellow tufts, the poles of the farmer's barbed-wire fence, and above that the gray sky dotted with birds seeking cover. She understood then that along with the money, and her grandfather's rubber company, they had been abandoned. To cheer her, Esme's mother promised her that they would open the bakery. They would spend the summer at the

Thimble Island cottage. They would visit the puppet theater that Esme loved. But her mother had soon felt the effects of the cancer that Esme had learned she'd inherited. Esme was almost thankful they never did any of the things her mother had promised.

The boat's movement was lulling. Esme felt the scotch settle in her limbs. Her mouth was numb. They came around a small turn and she pointed out the island, the house its only structure, surrounded by scrub pine and granite and thickets of blackberry. "That's the place," she said. Her great-grandmother's wild roses climbed a trellis. Two beech trees, brought over as saplings in the dinghy, flanked the house. Dean made a sound under his breath—"Oh," he said, and then the unspoken recognition. The attorney who met with her long ago had mentioned the developers and investors interested in the property. But Esme had no real need for money. Dean, who lived in town, probably knew that about her. She was comforted by the assumption he knew more about her than she could know herself. It was easier than having to explain.

Her grandmother had sent her to the Thimble Island house on an errand. The night before, Esme had opened a bottle of sherry and poured her grandmother a glass that remained untouched on the coffee table, and she'd told Esme to go back.

"You'll want to check the sideboard in the kitchen first," her grandmother said. "Then the breakfront, if it's not there."

"What am I going to look for, Nana?" Esme asked. She was humoring her at the time. They were sitting in the living room with one lamp lit. "Just look," her grandmother said. She wore her glasses on a chain. Her breasts were large and soft beneath her blouse. Esme remained perplexed. "Is it bigger than a bread box?" she asked.

And then her grandmother said a very odd thing. "Your father is bigger than a breadbox."

Caridad stood on the downstairs landing. She wore a peignoir decorated with tiny silk roses, one of her grandmother's that Esme used to dress up in as a child. "Nighty night time," Caridad said.

Alice squinted at Esme. "Who is she talking to?"

Esme helped her grandmother up off the couch. Her clothes smelled faintly sour. Esme didn't inquire any further about her grandmother's request. She didn't want to ruin her own hopes of what she had meant. She felt the mystery of the house on the island, a place she had allowed herself to forget. She believed in it now, felt it sustain her as Dean tied the boat at the dock. He would have helped her, but she was out before he could. Then, there was the awkwardness of the moment when they both knew her use for him had ended.

"No picnic lunch?" he said.

"I won't be long," she told him.

She started up the path to the porch, and glanced back.

Dean stood resolute by the launch and made no move to follow her. The cottage was a Victorian, built in 1870. It was never leased out to renters in the summer. There was someone to make sure the property didn't succumb to the elements. Esme stepped up onto the porch and fumbled with the key. She opened the red-painted screen door. She felt a little twist of apprehension, tightening with the spring's squeak. Behind her on the dock Dean waited with his arms folded, pretending not to watch. Esme imagined he'd report all of this that evening to the patrons in the lounge where they'd met. It would be a story made interesting only by his embellishments. Inside smelled of oil paint. The furniture was draped. Esme remembered the way the reflection off the water bounced around the living room. The house was clearly empty, and everything else she remembered was colored by her disappointment at finding it so—the old flecked bathroom mirror, the chip in the sink, the smell of kerosene, the sag in her bed, the sea slapping the rocks. The books on the shelves moldered. The fireplace mantle was lined with clamshells and periwinkles, jingles, arks and slippers, pale green sea glass, angel wings.

Esme had never understood her father's leaving. She saw him again that morning, smelled the shaving soap, saw him there in front of the mirror in the pale blue suit. His face was reddened and bloated. He smelled, too, of whatever he drank the night before, the liquor still coming off his skin. Her mother was asleep. It was only Esme and her father up at that hour. Outside the sky lightened. On the front lawn there was a little snow. Blackbirds came to peck at the places where the grass showed. She told him the suit was the color of the sky. *Just-spring*, she said. She was still very sad about her grandfather, but she could not say that.

"I'm a rich man," her father said. His shoes were polished, and he looked dashing. She could not imagine where he might be heading in such clothes. He did not put on "The Wreck of the Edmund Fitzgerald." She watched him go out the door into the garage. His leather soles tapped across the concrete. She watched him back out the car and smelled the exhaust, the way it came into the house, along with the smell of apples rotting in their crates, and the melting snow. The car left in a spiral of whitish fog. Esme thought of her grandfather in the Healey. She felt a terrible fear, standing at the bay window, watching her father leave. Don't hit a tree, she thought. Don't hit a tree. There was never any report of her father's death. The money, saved for years by her grandfather, and her grandfather's father, acquired from the eventual sale of the rubber company, became Esme's mother's. The two of them waited four years and never heard from him. Esme, the sole inheritor, waited eighteen more. Beyond the cottage windows the Sound churned black and green. The mist burned off under a pale sun. She went to the kitchen sideboard and undid the latch. Inside were mousetraps and wet matches and candles. There was an old bottle of sherry, the label peeling. On it was a gift tag dangling from gold string. *For Mother, with love and absolution, 1973.* Esme heard footsteps, and she knew that Dean had come into the house looking for her. She stood up with the bottle and turned to face him.

"That what she wanted?" he said, chuckling. He had his hands stuffed in his pockets. "Must be a good year."

Behind him the wind tapped the screen door against its frame. The water sloshed the rocks. Esme shrugged. "I don't really know what she wanted." She stood there with the bottle in her hand. Her father wasn't here, hiding out, waiting for the money she'd brought. There wasn't a boat tied in a hidden cove, its motor rumbling, ready for their escape. She found her legs were tired, and she sank to the floor with the bottle. She saw Dean's furtive glance to her bag on the floor where she'd dropped it. Her eyes were even with his knees, young and knobby, with a limited sense of the world. She had not bothered to find out what he had been doing in the seafood restaurant lounge that morning, but she saw now, clearly, that he'd been there to see Patsy, that the two of them were aligned, that when Esme had come in with her cash, wearing her mother's pearls, they had hatched a shaky plan to steal from her. Maybe they wanted to run away together, escape the little town with its briny smell and desperate, wealthy islanders. She remembered the look Patsy had given Dean at the bar, so like those her mother once gave her grandfather. Caution and love.

Esme motioned to the bag on the floor. "Just take it already," she said. And to her surprise he did. He bent from the waist and snatched it up, keeping his eyes on her. Esme heard his footsteps retreat across the wood floor. She heard the spring on the red-painted door. But the door didn't close, and she waited, imagining him hesitating, one foot on the porch. Then the door banged and she heard him return. He eased himself down on the floor across from her and leaned against the plaster wall. He took off his hat and set it beside him. He kept the bag secure in his lap. Esme saw he was waiting, watching her.

"I tried for once to be the person who was gone," she told him, "rather than the one left behind."

He considered this. He tipped his head up and stared at the ceiling. "Someday," he said, his voice steady and low as if someone might be listening, "there will be nothing left but the rock the house stands on."

"You think I should open the sherry," she said.

"I think that as far as you know, after all this time, your father might still be somewhere," he said.

Around them the drapes on the furniture flapped. The sea breeze flew through, heavy and damp. Without looking underneath, Esme knew the tables that stood on turned wooden legs, the chairs' upholstered laps worn to the shape of the people who sat in them. Maybe her father had chosen to live a life that had forked off, like a path, or a tree branch—the way leading to others, to narrower branches, to twigs and stems and then, untraceably, the blissful confusion of leaves. Dean, despite his mutinous heart, was trying to be kind. He'd assumed the worst thing would be to die. But Esme knew otherwise. Around her the swept sand filled the floorboard cracks. The knife that cut cocktail limes left its imprint on the Formica counter. The tide rose up to the marker on the rock. The mattresses waited for their stained sheets. Her grandmother dove from the granite ledge in her bathing cap, slender legs straight, feet lifted, caught in midair by a camera's shutter. Outside clouds moved and the sun blinked like a faulty bulb. Not quite there, not quite here.

The Fountain

After the divorce, Mrs. Moriarity found herself bereft of anyone who would call her by her first name. The younger people, like the teenager who mowed the lawn, or the neighbor's child sent over with some of her mail, called her Mrs. Moriarity out of an honest disinterest. Phone solicitors and store clerks did it to create professional distance, and the religious witnesses, going door to door with their pamphlets, needed to counterbalance their personal concern for her soul. Some, the rakish ones who knew both her husband and her new situation, like the dry cleaner owner, Joe Lombardi, or the mechanic at the dealership where she brought her constantly dented Mercedes, said her name with a sarcastic grin, as if suddenly the possibility existed that they might have her naked on their Polylux satin sheets, or spread out on the backseats of their Crown Victorias.

Mrs. Moriarity was not unattractive, or old, but Mr. Moriarity had left her six months ago for a younger replica of herself—a dark-eyed, dark-haired girl in her twenties, who had a lush mouth, a less jaded expression, and to whom all of Mrs. Moriarity's friends had swarmed. Mrs. Moriarity assumed the guise that she was not affected by the ordeal of the divorce, or the absence of Mr. Moriarity, his abrupt manner of speaking, the swishing noise he made putting on his suit jacket in the morning. She told herself she expected he would move on. He had left his previous wife for her ten years before. She had plenty of money, and she had just purchased an older Spanish-style house in need of some restoration, on a street darkened by the overhang of live oaks. Her only concern, lately, had been that she had not found anyone else.

She had opportunities—the lawyer who handled her divorce, the banker who opened her new account. These were men, divorced themselves, whose white cuffs showed beyond their suit sleeves, who stacked her paperwork speaking warmly and formally while their eyes, nearly pleading, pressed other intentions. They would bring her to restaurants, to gatherings and functions, lead her on their arms back into her old life. The prospect dangled like a shiny lure, but she did not take it. In the world of pairings and trysts and illicit gropings, she went untouched and alone, like a penitent. Until the afternoon she pulled into the drive-thru nursery, she existed in a kind of sexual limbo, eyeing the tanned and hairless chest of the teenager who trimmed her podocarpus.

The nursery was ten minutes outside downtown Tampa, off a four-lane boulevard. It had no business name advertised, but the owner had placed fuchsia flowered hibiscus and glossy variegated ginger by the curb with a big handwritten placard that said, "Buy One, Get One Free." There was no real road to drive through, but a grassy area worn by tire tracks that passed along the side of the property and exited in back, on a side street. Midway down, an RV sat under a large, blooming golden rain tree. She stopped at this and waited for someone to emerge and provide service.

The expressway passed close by, and the cars' tires made a constant humming sound. Mrs. Moriarity waited a long time. She had nothing else to do, and she wanted the ginger for an empty bed near her front door. Eventually, she got out of the car and stood in the shade of the tree, her heels sinking into the dirt. She considered hitting the horn. She thought she might go up and tap on the door, but just then it flew open with a hurried impatience, as if the latch had stuck, and Martin Speed came out. He was tall and lean, with a closely trimmed cap of disheveled, prematurely white hair, and he had to bend his head to fit through the door. He started talking at once, both apologetic and frazzled, caught off-guard, his Hawaiian print shirt flapping unbuttoned as if he'd just put it on. His brown eyes were bright, the skin on his face damp. He gave off the odor and sheen of having been caught in the middle of something sexual, and she looked behind him to the door of the RV, watching for someone else to come out, but no one did. He wore grubby khaki cargo shorts, and he fumbled in one of his deep pockets, pulled out a pack of Pall Mall cigarettes, and quickly lit one.

"I want the ginger," Mrs. Moriarity said.

He looked at her. He had a way of standing with his cigarette between two fingers that made her think of an old nightclub comedian, spotlighted in front of a microphone, his head enshrouded in cigarette smoke, about to deliver a line.

"What do you want it for?" he asked. He smiled at her, almost a smirk. The cigarette in his hand shook. He smelled, faintly, of whiskey.

Later, Mrs. Moriarity would determine that there were things that initially flustered them both—his penetrating look, his exposed chest, her silver Mercedes, gleaming in the rutted path, her clothing, beige and expensive, the kind she always wore in her life with Mr. Moriarity, and her manner, which did not fit the clothing or the car, that came from her life before, when she was a cocktail waitress in the lounge with red velvet booths, where men like Mr. Moriarity met their girlfriends, and she had schemed, much as Martin Speed schemed then, to have whatever she could of it all.

"Well," she said. "I have an empty bed."

And Martin Speed grinned. "I'm sorry to hear that," he said.

Mrs. Moriarity felt her face redden. Martin nudged her with his shoulder, shaking his head at her. They went up front and he picked out two plants and loaded them in her trunk. She wrote him a check and he gave her one of his cards, explaining that his real interest was landscape design, that if she found she needed help with hers, she could call. She smiled and assured him she just might, got into her car, and started it up. He stepped back with the check in one hand, the other searching out another cigarette in his shorts pocket. She saw him glance at the check and look back up.

"Have a nice afternoon, Amber," he said, his face eager and hopeful, his thin shoulders hunched in the Hawaiian shirt. She knew, to him, she was a potential windfall, and the idea amused her. She liked how her name sounded when he said it, not the sloe-eyed slutty girl named after a romance novel's heroine, not even the woman that Mr. Moriarity took to fund-raisers for the Florida Aquarium. Martin Speed offered her the chance to be anyone she chose, opportunities opened up and fanned out in front of her.

She set his card on her kitchen counter, on top of the growing stack of contractors' cards. She intended to call him, but after a few days had passed she half-forgot him. She was busy dealing with painters and the people sanding the floors, workmen with wild hair and glassy eyes, high on fumes and the joint she caught them smoking in the verdant area by her trash cans. She spent days dodging calls from Rita Worthy, a friend from her married life, whose desire to get together and catch up on things like they used to seemed sad and nostalgic and so unlike Rita that her motives made Mrs. Moriarity suspicious. So, it was a week before she called Martin Speed. She had set the ginger plants by the front door in their black plastic pots, but hadn't planted them, and when he arrived in his battered white van and came up the front walk, he stopped and looked at them. He had on a different flowered print shirt, buttoned up this time. Mrs. Moriarity had watched him walk along her front path, his quick assessment of the neighborhood, her house and the yard, just a glance around, like a dog sensing something in the air. She met him on the front porch.

"Well?" she asked.

Martin took some steps back and furrowed his brow. "At least you didn't plant it yet," he said. He laughed and pulled out his rumpled pack of Pall Malls.

She held out her hand. "Can I bum one of those?"

Martin gave her a cigarette and stepped forward with his lighter. From within the folds of his shirt she smelled his skin. He slid a breath mint around in his mouth. They stood out on the front lawn, smoking, and Mrs. Moriarity began imagining what might happen after she invited him inside, when someone drove up in an old turquoise Chevy truck that continued to chug and cough after he'd turned it off. He was young, with ropey muscles, and long, curly brown hair. His dark eyes had circles of exhaustion under them. His jeans were covered with white plaster dust, and he stood by the truck and clomped his work boots and shook the dust out of his hair. He came up to them on the lawn and stood a ways apart from Martin Speed, who introduced him to Mrs. Moriarity as his partner, Cicero.

"I'm kind of a mess," Cicero said. Small gold hoops hung from both his earlobes. He smiled at Mrs. Moriarity, wiping his hands on his pants.

They had brought a scrapbook of other jobs they'd done, and they sat inside at the wide-planked kitchen table under the brass chandelier and perused the before and after photos. Cicero's talents were revealed in a customer's gazebo, a built-in patio grill, fences and latticed arbors and a waterfall over a garden grotto, though he sat silent and almost sullen through most of it. Mrs. Moriarity served imported beer, and Martin Speed worked her over with his feng shui. She let him lead her outside, where he commented on the color of the front door, the symmetry of the arches, the necessity of keeping the balance between the selected plants based on their texture and smell and color. Mrs. Moriarity nodded, glancing toward Cicero, who followed them around the house, keeping a few paces back, his arms folded over his chest. Every so often he would meet her gaze and then look down at his boots.

It was an October evening, the shadows deep and somber under the live oaks, the air heavy with the smell of suburbia: gasoline, mown grass, fabric softener effused from upstairs dryer vents, freshly brewed gourmet coffee, curry and coriander, the result of the woman next door's attempt at Indian cuisine. Mrs. Moriarity bummed another cigarette. Martin eagerly reached into his pants.

"Have you lived here long?" he asked.

Mrs. Moriarity told him she'd just moved in. She had wanted the house the moment she saw it, she said. It filled the length of the property, its arched front porch long and stately. Below the tiled roofline ran an elaborate plasterwork cornice, and a concrete angel medallion hung over the front door—a face with heavy lidded eyes surrounded by curving wings. Through an arched gateway on the side of the house, in a courtyard covered by a grape arbor, resided a ruined fountain with the same angel motif. The exterior needed stucco work, and a new coat of paint. Inside, the oak flooring, which had been damaged by termites, was in the process of repair, as were some of the plaster walls marred by an undetected leak in the roof. None of this bothered Mrs. Moriarity. The house had a ballroom with a vaulted ceiling she considered painting pale blue. When she climbed the brick steps onto the porch, when she moved through the doorway into the house, she felt something old and interminable she could not have described to anyone else, even Martin Speed, who seemed just then, standing smoking and watching her, to be deliberating some elaborate punch line.

"And Mr. Moriarity is . . . ?" he asked.

"Right now, probably offering the new Mrs. Moriarity a Caribbean vacation or a pair of Prada boots," she told him.

Martin, she saw, held his amusement in check. He looked into her eyes, searching for things: vulnerability, anger, jealousy, sadness, none of which he would see, she was confident.

"I can't imagine that ever being you," he said, as if he had her pegged.

Her neighbors' husbands' cars returned, one by one, home from the office, or a hospital shift, or the golf course, or the hushed dimness of a restaurant bar before the dinner hour, or the air-conditioned dampness of a motel on Gandy Boulevard. They eased into their spots in the driveways, and she heard the subtle sounds of engines cutting off, leather-soled footfalls on the concrete.

"Well, sometimes," she told him, "you be who you have to be."

And Martin made a sound of protest. "I wouldn't know anything about that," he said, thoughtfully. Cicero, standing behind him, looked up at the darkening sky, and in the growing brightness of the streetlights' halogen mist Mrs. Moriarity thought she saw him roll his eyes. They came around to the courtyard, where the leaves on the grapevine had begun to brown and wither. The fountain stood with its chipped basin mottled and slick with mold, its angel's missing nose. Cicero walked around it, suddenly interested. He squatted down at the pedestal base and prodded the loose concrete, sifted through the layer of dead grape leaves. Mrs. Moriarity watched him, only half listening to Martin Speed's pitch—something about the luck of the eastern exposure, the pattern of the existing terra-cotta tiles, the contrast of the black gate against the white wall.

Cicero stood and pulled out his own cigarette, a Marlboro. "This can be fixed," he said. Mrs. Moriarity knew it was the first well-intentioned thing that had been said all evening.

"I wondered about that," she told him. "It seems sad to leave it like this."

Something passed between Martin and Cicero. In the fading light, Mrs. Moriarity couldn't make it out. She looked back and forth between the two of them, an undercurrent of tightly wound silence encircling them both. Cicero had his hands on his hips. He blew his cigarette smoke up past the remains of grapes, past the arbor's wooden lattice, into the night sky, the beginnings of stars. Martin's expression resembled the apprehension of a parent watching a child about to misbehave. He looked toward Mrs. Moriarity, his jaw tightening. "Why don't we work up a price for everything," he said, the brightness in his voice forced. "Then, we'll call you, say, tomorrow afternoon?"

Cicero turned to face Martin, and Mrs. Moriarity saw his smile, false and quick. He dropped his cigarette onto the terracotta tiles and stubbed it out with his boot. She sensed that Martin Speed's game was not one Cicero was keen to play, his mention of the fountain some diversion from the plan, a form of rebellion. She saw, too, that despite this, he was bound to Martin by something she did not yet understand. Part of it had to do with money and the things it afforded, but not totally. As they headed around to the driveway in front, as the two men separated and climbed into their vehicles and backed out, she wondered if Cicero saw beyond the ease and grace of Martin Speed's comedian's timing, if he shared, as she once did, his desperate wish to become something greater in the eyes of the world.

When Mrs. Moriarity was younger, working in the cocktail lounge, she learned that different people respected different things. She was the best waitress in the place because she took the time to read the customers, to learn what they liked. Mr. Moriarity liked people to know what he wanted, to give it to him as quickly as possible, without distraction—double oldfashioned, made with Old Overholt rye. He was impressed when she remembered his girlfriend's drink, and once, when she had brought the drinks to the table, and the girlfriend had demurred and requested something else, he became irritated, and never brought her back. After that, he came alone and one night when she brought his drink over he had grabbed her arm, a very unlikely move for him.

"There's something about you," he said. He had a low voice, roughened by the Old Overholt. His eyebrows were threaded with gray, and underneath, his eyes held a deep searching sadness she was too young to notice at the time.

She had stuck one hip out and smiled at him, confident and pleased. "Don't be so sure you know what you want," he cautioned.

Later, after they married, Mr. Moriarity told her the story of his accumulation of wealth. At the time, she believed he was telling her how alike they were, that he had satisfied his own desire just as she had satisfied hers. During the course of their marriage, she continued to believe that Mr. Moriarity had never wanted anything else but the money he'd earned and the things it afforded him. She worried now, as she closed her front door and greeted the unnamed presence in her house, its smell and vibration, that she had been wrong, that what they'd wanted had been different things altogether, and because she had been too satisfied herself, she had not sought deep enough or been sure enough for Mr. Moriarity. In her drawing room, French doors faced the courtyard where the fountain stood, dry and enveloped in darkness, a mist growing around it. Mrs. Moriarity opened the doors and stood there and listened to the grape leaves rustle. Behind her the house was still and dark; she knew she would walk through it now, her footsteps sounding on the newly finished floors, and turn on a few lamps. She might sit at her piano or lie prone on one of her Persian rugs and stare up at the ballroom's high vault imagining it as the sky. The happiness she found in this place, with these things, she could not deny. But she sensed at that moment that she would never forget completely the resonance of Mr. Moriarity's voice, the simple longing she had felt bringing drinks to patrons in the velvet booths, and these would always suggest, like the separation of particles in the mist, something lost.

The next day Martin Speed brought the quote by. She barely glanced at it. They stood out in the driveway, and Martin explained to her a special deal he was offering some of his better clients. If they paid in advance he would give them a 15 percent discount, which would provide her large and barren yard with more plants for the same amount.

"We could do a bank of rosemary in the courtyard, some climbing jasmine on those walls," he told her, his eyes bright, his white hair combed neatly to one side.

Mrs. Moriarity wrote him another check. As she did she speculated what he might do with the money, the celebration that would begin the moment he left her driveway, and regretted only that she would not be part of it. She remembered the first large tip Mr. Moriarity gave her, tucked neatly under his empty glass on her tray. Mrs. Moriarity felt a certain power in granting Martin this kind of happiness, though she could not deny that much of it came from the indebtedness she believed he would now feel. She forgot that she had taken Mr. Moriarity's money, spent it as lavishly as if she had found it blown into debris at a curbside, without any thought to its ties, the traces it looped around her neck and shoulders, like a harness.

Martin had promised to begin work in two days, but when a week passed, and neither he nor Cicero had appeared, she drove over to the nursery, down the rutted path, and parked near the RV. Mrs. Moriarity turned off her car, opened the door, and stepped out. She heard the cars on the expressway, their shuddering passage moving all the green leaves on the nursery plants. She did not wait this time but marched over the ruts of the path, over the scattered hibiscus petals to the RV door, and knocked. When Martin didn't answer she tried the door, grasping the latch handle, giving it a small tug. Quietly, unexpectedly, it opened and she glanced inside at the dismal, close interior, the floor littered with tracked-in dirt and crushed rain tree pods. The light from outside seemed to seep in, the pinkish orange of the golden rain tree. Something fell onto the roof, a tiny hollow pinging noise that startled her, though she could see that Martin wasn't there.

The RV smelled of cigarettes and spilled liquor and the tramped-in soil. She had not been sure if he actually lived in the RV, and now she realized that he did. There were his shirts, an array of prints hung on a rod down at one end, an expensive-looking stainless pot on a single burner, a damp towel hung on a door-knob. A cockroach skittered across the small Formica counter. Mrs. Moriarity stepped into the RV and shut the door. Around her, in what looked like a flea market's disarray, were items she knew could not be Martin's—a woman's sequined evening gown, a Cuisinart food processor, leather-bound books, a library globe, a miniature oil of a man in nineteenth-century clothes, a velvet case that held, she knew without opening it, Towle silver. On the kitchen counter were plastic vials—Valium and Xanax and Demerol, prescribed for someone else. She knew there would be jewelry as well, maybe tucked away under the cushioned bunk, and she remembered, uneasily, her first apartment, just a sparely furnished room in a house, how she had worked private parties for the owner of the cocktail lounge, bartending, sometimes, at the homes of his patrons, and had taken things herself, perusing bureau drawers, riffling through closets. The things she'd taken had been small, like talismans to represent the life she wanted—cuff links, or a silver compact, a silk camisole rolled to fit in the palm of her hand.

She had intended to find Martin in the nursery and approach him about the plants. "Martin," she'd planned to say, "what about creating a pathway for my energy?" gauging his response, his sly smile, his arm thrown over her shoulder to pull her in with unabashed tenderness. Now, the silence inside the RV, the airlessness, the orange tint, were heady, and she moved over to the built-in bunk and sat down and listened to her own breathing. Beyond the RV walls the hibiscus and mandeville bloomed on trellises, jasmine in five-gallon buckets threaded its way into ficus limbs. She heard footsteps approach, heard the door in its frame, and Martin Speed came in. He did not seem surprised to see her there, and later she realized that he'd seen her car, that he suspected where she was after a quick search of the nursery grounds. At the time, standing in the doorway, he seemed oddly calm. They regarded each other like criminals facing capture, each with a mind for escape they did not want to reveal to the other.

"I'm sorry," Mrs. Moriarity said, shaken, the heat of the RV making her weak.

Martin reached into his pocket and pulled out a cigarette and lit it up.

"I'm not," he said, his brown eyes uncharacteristically somber.

Mrs. Moriarity, afterward, wondered what he'd meant. Had she assumed he knew she was there about the plants? Later, she could not remember if the issue of the plants ever came up. He had kissed her first, or she had stood and gone to him. Neither was clear. His mouth had tasted of whiskey and the cigarette. Her arms, reaching around to clasp him to her, found his back hard and unyielding, all bones and muscles. She realized she had not held anyone since Mr. Moriarity, whose back, padded with age, had been familiar and soft. Sex with Mr. Moriarity had been transactional, a formal bartering in which she kept her self safe, always with something to be gained. But pressed to the bunk mattress by Martin Speed's hips, his hands sliding up beneath her blouse, her clothes shed in a pile on the dirty floor, Mrs. Moriarity could not tell who would owe whom, and afterward, Martin silently watching her dress, pulling her toward him for a lingering kiss before she left, she realized nothing at all had been said. For a week, while she waited for a word from him, while she drove to the grocery store, or watered her potted geraniums, the scene replayed itself, and still, she could not tell if she had gotten what she wanted.

It was not Martin Speed but Cicero who showed up on a Friday at eight a.m. while Mrs. Moriarity was on the phone with Rita Worthy. She had easily avoided her calls, but since the afternoon with Martin she had begun to feel untethered and alone, and this feeling had prompted her to answer the phone and then agree to spend the weekend with Rita visiting antique stores in Mt. Dora. She watched through the French doors as Cicero came through the arched gateway and crossed the courtyard. He wore olive green work pants that hung off his hips, and a white t-shirt through which she could see the indentation of his ribs. He walked around the fountain, as he had before, smoking a cigarette. He stood out there so long that Mrs. Moriarity felt slightly deviant, watching him, so she tapped on the glass and opened the door to make herself known. Cicero smiled and waved, and she went outside. The sun slipped over the edge of the courtyard wall. It was a hazy morning, and already warm. Cicero asked her questions about the house—what year it was built, who lived in it before. Mrs. Moriarity offered him coffee, and she smoked a few of his cigarettes, both of them avoiding the mention of Martin.

Cicero told her he liked the architecture, and they sat down on the concrete step and looked at the fountain. Mrs. Moriarity asked where he was from. When he was ten years old, he said, the man he thought was his father told him he was mistaken. Cicero had been conceived in Spain while his mother was there alone, on a writer's retreat. It had been his birth, much earlier than expected, that led to questions of paternity, and the eventual divorce. He had grown up in Michigan, living in one of four of his parents' combined residences, all of this very confusing for a small boy. As a young teenager he had befriended the wrong kind of people and ended up in juvenile hall under an agreement, arranged by his mother through her influential ex-husband, that allowed him to go home in the evenings to sleep, provided he returned each morning for incarceration. Cicero told her these things with a sardonic smile, carefully reading her reaction.

"I left when I was eighteen," he said.

"Do you hear from them?" she asked.

"I get a check," he told her, "when they find out where I am. But I always tear it up. I don't want their fucking money."

A grape leaf, large and brown and buoyed on an invisible current, drifted to their feet. Mrs. Moriarity reached over and touched his shoulder.

"Your father might have been a bullfighter," she said.

Cicero ducked his head and shook it back and forth, laughing. His eyes were clear and calm. He flexed his hands and laid them on his thighs.

"You sound like my girlfriend," he said.

"Oh," she said. She realized he thought she was flirting with him, and she wondered, then, if she had been. Something in her voice made him turn and stare at her, and then he reached out and lifted a piece of her hair from her face, leaving Mrs. Moriarity with a feeling of breathless disquiet. He stood up and excused himself to get his tools, shuffling through the courtyard and around front to his truck. He worked for four hours tirelessly in the hot sun. At noon, a blue compact car pulled into the drive. Mrs. Moriarity thought at first it was the maid. But then Cicero came around to the car to meet the girl who got out and gave him something in a brown paper bag, put her arms around his shoulders, and pressed her large breasts up against his chest. The girlfriend, Mrs. Moriarity decided.

Her name was Pammy. That afternoon she wore her hair plaited in two braids, which, along with the freckles on her nose, made her look younger than she really was. Mrs. Moriarity thought this later, sitting across from her at the kitchen table. She had invited them in, and Cicero had eaten the sandwich that Pammy had brought him, and Mrs. Moriarity had given them beer, and they'd all stayed in the kitchen for a while, Pammy and Cicero talking about the house they were renovating, and Mrs. Moriarity listening, smiling, nodding her head, thinking instead about the two of them together. While Pammy talked, her voice high and thin and childish, she moved her hands over Cicero's shoulders, along his neck, up into his hair. She placed a hand on his thigh. Cicero kept his own hands on the tabletop, polite and awkward, as if in front of Mrs. Moriarity he felt self-conscious about revealing that he and Pammy had sex.

Later, after Cicero had gone back out to work, Mrs. Moriarity opened a bottle of Chardonnay, and she and Pammy smoked Cicero's cigarettes, sat out in two iron chaises in the backyard by the empty flower beds. Pammy rolled her shorts up high on her legs. When she leaned forward to talk, her bra strap slipped down her arm, and she slid it up deftly with her thumb.

"You heard," Pammy said. "About what happened last week?" She widened her eyes, and the fine lines around them smoothed out. She had reapplied glimmering lip gloss, pulled from her shorts pocket, and her face, animated when she spoke, took on the appearance of mock surprise. Mrs. Moriarity said she hadn't heard anything. Pammy told her how she had to go down to the police station and pick the two of them up—Martin and Cicero, last Friday night. Mrs. Moriarity imagined a discovery of the RV's contents, the nursery roped off with yellow police tape. Pammy hesitated, keeping her in suspense.

"They had a fight," she said quietly, almost under her breath. "A falling out."

"About what?" Mrs. Moriarity asked. She imagined an argument, come to blows in some lowly public place.

Pammy made a face. "You never know with them." She smoked her cigarette dreamily, looking around the yard.

"Don't you want to know?" Mrs. Moriarity said.

Pammy shrugged. "This is a pretty yard," she said, sighing, glancing at Mrs. Moriarity out of the corner of her eye.

Martin Speed had still not shown up, and Mrs. Moriarity, trying to sound unconcerned, said something about his absence. Pammy turned, propped herself up on one arm, her freckled nose twitching.

"Are you in love with Martin?" she asked.

Mrs. Moriarity felt a sense of foreboding. Pammy watched her, the empty Chardonnay glass balanced on her hip.

"Why would I be?" Mrs. Moriarity asked.

Pammy sighed again and flopped back down. "Oh, everyone is at one point or another," she said. She stubbed her cigarette out in the grass and got to her feet. She put her hands over her head and stretched, turned to glance over her shoulder at Cicero, his T-shirted back to them, wet with perspiration.

"He won't even pay him for this, you know," she said.

Mrs. Moriarity and Pammy both stood on the dry lawn and looked at each other.

"He already spent the money you gave him," Pammy told her, almost bitterly.

Mrs. Moriarity had suspected as much. Still, she felt a small lurch of disappointment, an almost mild surprise. She had, she realized, expected Martin to come anyway. She wondered suddenly if Martin and Cicero's argument had been about her, and then Pammy stepped forward and put her arms around her shoulders and held her, as she had Cicero earlier that afternoon. The pressure of Pammy's arms pulled her in so that she could feel the girl's breasts, the bones of her ribs, smell the artificial citrus scent of her shampoo. Pammy let go and stepped away. She gave Mrs. Moriarity a disarmingly sincere smile, one prompted by pity, intended to bolster her. Then she turned and headed around to the driveway toward her car, her braids swinging, her shorts still rolled up on her thighs.

Mrs. Moriarity went inside, Pammy's embrace lingering on the skin of her collarbones, along the arch of her neck. She watched Cicero through the French doors. He had brought a pump, which he was installing in a hollow near the pedestal base. He had started to build a nose for the angel, and had brought cans of spray paint that simulated the texture of stone. She saw that he and Pammy had taken her side, that they believed Martin had betrayed her, and she had been made a fool. But she was no more worthy of Cicero's labor than Martin. The money meant nothing. It was Mr. Moriarity's money, given to her monthly to grant his freedom, and she felt, unlike Cicero dodging his parents' checks, paid off for some mistake in love. She was still unsure what she had expected from Martin, and so she could not tell if things were even between them, though she sensed that somehow, something had been overlooked, that she had been deprived of some closeness she thought she'd paid for but, really, did not know how to earn.

She watched Cicero tidy up his tools, set them in an out-of-the-way spot for when he returned, and she wanted to tell him to take the tools, to never mind the fountain. He caught her watching him, and she started, but he smiled and held up his pack of cigarettes, and she went out into the courtyard to smoke with him. He told her that he would finish up on Monday, unless he found time during the weekend to work. Mrs. Moriarity, reminded with a sinking feeling of her promise to Rita, told him not to worry, she would be gone for the weekend anyway. She let him light her cigarette, let her silence in the falling evening seem nothing more than a preference, and not the troubled incapability of words.

She left the next morning, driving at Rita's suggestion. Rita was a woman Mr. Moriarity had often flirted with, something that had never bothered Mrs. Moriarity in the old days, but things were different now, she learned, as Rita chattered on, her manicured nails catching the light, her perfume settling into the leather upholstery. Rita Worthy had been spurned, probably for the same overt poses, the nearly exposed breasts and inappropriate touches that she had always exhibited, and she was eager to form a bond with Mrs. Moriarity on the subject of the new Mrs. Moriarity—a woman who sat on her husband's lap in front of guests, who asked him, "Baby, can I get you another drink?" or "Baby, take me home now, it's late." Mrs. Moriarity thought that her replacement was a much better actress than she had been. She realized she could now say this, and more, that she and Rita could strike up a new friendship based on this common interest. But she saw, too, the possibility that Mr. Moriarty's new wife loved him, that he had finally found what he wanted, and she could not even pretend to be resentful. She listened, silent and annoyed, until a stop at a rest area, when she finally turned to Rita.

"I don't really care about any of this," Mrs. Moriarty said.

Rita quieted. "I don't like your tone," she said.

They sat in the car staring out the windshield, the space widening between them, and Rita suggested that the weekend might have been a bad idea, and Mrs. Moriarty agreed, pulled out onto the interstate, and headed home. Rita said nothing during the return trip, plotting, Mrs. Moriarty knew, to spread rumors and form other bonds based on this refusal of friendship. In the driveway, retrieving her bag from the trunk, she gave Mrs. Moriarty an angry glare that let her know she had lost all possible ties to her old life.

Driving to her house, Mrs. Moriarty felt numbed by apprehension. She almost turned toward the drive-thru nursery, almost pulled into the rutted drive, intent on demanding what she paid for, but it was too disturbing to her now, what she had hoped to pay for. She understood how Mr. Moriarty had felt, how he had continued to hope that she might become someone other than a woman he had purchased for her body and her youth, and some steadfast, intent look of promise in her expression, the look he had come to dream would deliver love. It was nearly dark when she pulled onto her street, the sky still reflective and deeply blue. She saw their cars lining her drive—Cicero's and Pammy's and Martin Speed's, pulled all the way up to avoid any obvious detection from the neighborhood. She thought, "Of course," and felt a spark of hope, and a kind of happiness, and then a shadow of misgiving. She parked alongside Cicero's truck at the top of the driveway and let herself in through the kitchen door. She could hear them in the drawing room, their voices low and teasing, and beyond this something else, a sound colored with iridescence. She approached the drawing room and made them out. They had the French doors open to the courtyard, and she heard, quite clearly now, the fountain, its water sound soft and lulling. Martin and Cicero stood in the doorway of the unlit room, the outlines of them still clear against the chrome blue of the sky. Pammy sat on the couch, her hair in blond waves over her shoulders. They each held one of her Baccarat wine goblets, and they were laughing, their differences, if they ever existed, reconciled now over Mr. Moriarity's '82 Château Haut-Brion. Beneath the sound of the fountain, their laughter was laden with attraction. Mrs. Moriarity watched Martin Speed place his arm around Cicero's neck and pull him toward his chest, a boyish, intimate tug of affection, and Mrs. Moriarity said nothing, drawn into the high, vibrating tension of the room. Pammy saw her first. Her eyes formed a widened stare, ready to proclaim her innocence. Cicero faced her next, his expression shifting slightly to acknowledge her presence, his arms with their taut muscles looped around Martin Speed's waist.

Mrs. Moriarity walked up to the doorway alongside them and looked out at the fountain. She could feel Martin Speed beside her, the heat of his body under the printed shirt's flimsy fabric. The water spilled from the angel's mouth. The nose, she saw, had been crafted to resemble Cicero's own, a fine, sharp Spanish nose that suited the angel's lidded eyes, its long, waving hair, its feathered wings. She stood there for a time, listening to the water pooling in the basin, feeling the stir of bodies behind her, their movements charging the air. She heard a sip from a glass, the crystal being placed casually on a tabletop. She felt a flicker of anxiety. There was, after all, no Mr. Moriarity handing out whiskey sours, sitting in their midst with his level head and clear-cut expectations. She was adrift, and she knew, suddenly, she wanted to fall into someone's arms.

Mrs. Moriarity turned, the moment suspended within the fountain's water sound. She knew they wanted to continue drinking her wine, maybe choosing a room in which to have sex, that no matter how close to her they had pretended to be it was not enough to allow this breach, and they would look to Martin, eye each other, realizing the necessity of making amends. She would wait, her loneliness tapped, brimming, and let them decide what these would be, in what manner, and by whom.

Passing

We have come here on instinct, moved by a kind of nostalgic ache and a warmth in the air that lets us shed our clothes, jacket first, then shoes, until barefoot in cold, wet grass, we find ourselves waiting for something to happen, like migrating birds that fill and sway the power lines. Derby L. is with us. We drive his '55 Chevy, black as night with the flash of flames in the back. It is past midnight when we dive down the steep hill in town and circle the lake. I slide toward the open car window on red vinyl seats that smell of mildew, and listen to the chug-chug of the engine echo off the still water.

Keely will not look. She is up front next to Derby, clinging to his arm. The houses along the lake are small, on stilts. Their porch lights glow, rimmed with blue. The water of the lake is a dark, empty space, dotted with light. I see Keely turn toward it. We look at each other and our eyes say it, "Daddy," quickly, then forget.

"Turn the car around," Keely says. She yanks her arm away from Derby, and though I cannot see her face I know already the forehead lines under her bangs, the way her mouth twists with enough mild disgust to contradict her eyes, her eyes so full of something else, he may wonder, looking at them, if it is just the lake's reflections that make them shine.

"Why?" Derby asks.

"Never mind," I tell him.

"Turn around," Keely shouts. We are not drunk anymore. The party is miles away in another town. My husband is there, still, or he is home by now, eating something in front of the TV with his feet propped up on my new Hitchcock table and all the lights on. Derby swivels in his seat and looks at me through tinted aviator glasses. We barely know each other. I stop myself from reaching out and moving his long stringy hair from his face.

"We'll go to George's house, okay?" I say.

Keely is quiet. She folds her arms across her chest.

Derby touches her shoulder. "Good girl," he says. He lifts his glasses and asks, "Which way?" The skin around his eyes is swollen and red, as if he has been crying.

We circle the lake again. Our cousin George lives in a cedar-shingled house facing the water. His dog barks at us when we pull in. Derby L. shuffles right up to him in his motorcycle boots and pats his head. I have to pull Keely from the car.

"He's going to be mad at us," she says. "We didn't even call." She glances at Derby and says in my ear, "He's going to think we're crazy."

"I heard that," Derby says behind us in the dark, his voice high pitched, mimicking, under the clumping of his boots.

This is not the first time we have come back. Our mother lives here, in the same blue-gray house we grew up in. We come to visit her for the day and she is always outside, sitting in knee-high grass planting things, or walking through the neighborhood with her knotted brown cane, leaning on it, limping a little. The cane had always been an ornament propped beside the fireplace. I don't know why she began using it, because she is not as old as she pretends. When she looks at you, her face is smooth and white, beatific, like the face of the insane. We sit with her in the yard. When we have to go inside, we follow her, and we do not touch the things in the house—the photographs, the books, cabinet handles, doorknobs. Everything is the same, dusted, intact, as if we are waiting to start our lives over again when our father comes back. He left when I was fifteen and Keely twelve, and I can remember only the loss of him that lurked in my mother's bland look, her absent nod, the hands that dried themselves over and over on the dish towel, and then the faces of neighbors, pitying, curious, and their food, in white CorningWare casseroles, that arrived for years because no one knew when to stop. Still, we see these clean dishes stacked on the kitchen counter, and I think our mother must never cook.

In our house his absence was so forcibly felt, it was like an unidentifiable smell that followed you from room to room, and I could not stay there. Keely left soon after, pushed out, snubbed by the loss of him, unable to stand the smell of it that we have come close to naming—a mixture of oranges and freshly cut grass. I have never missed him. I do not remember the sound of his voice. When people ask me about him, I tell them he is dead.

"He's at the bottom of the lake," I say. We are sitting outside on George's dock. George is not home. Keely tells me to shut up. I can tell she is embarrassed for me, for the way I hide, so convincingly, in unreality.

"Yeah?" Derby L. says. "How'd that happen?" We are drinking George's beer, which we found in the refrigerator on the porch. Derby sits with his back against a wooden pile, peeling the label off the bottle. He looks up at me, waiting. He has taken his glasses off and his eyes are clear and dark like the surface of the lake. Keely glares at me.

"They think he killed himself," I say. "They found the boat out there." It was George's dinghy, the white fiberglass one with *Oh-My* painted on the front.

"No body!" Keely cries. "No body!" She stands up suddenly and pushes her face toward me. We are like teenagers again, arguing over the kitchen table, as if these are the roles we're to play for life, screaming uselessly over the blue flowered cloth and the bowl of waxed fruit, over our mother's bowed head, the startling, white nape of her neck, her empty eyes staring down at her hands. Her hands are tiny, veined, clutching each other. My sister and I are huge, like our father. We are too big for the small house. We shake the walls, fragile with shelved porcelain birds, fighting, throwing hairbrushes and shampoo bottles. We cannot solve the thing. No letter arrives. There isn't a phone call or a message from anyone. They drag the lake and find some other man and a woman in a steel-gray Toronado, pulled up from the depths dripping, their mouths in Os with teeth showing, bodies soft white, leaning against each other, full of water.

"It wasn't him," Keely says.

"They said it wasn't," I tell Derby. "They did tests."

We watched the whole thing through binoculars from this very spot. George was with us. It was spring then, too, but different, already hot, the air heavy and still, smelling of damp earth and decay. No one skied on the lake that summer, as if they did not want to risk showing disrespect by running over the body, bloated and baking on the black surface like an old log.

"What about the boat, then?" Derby asks. He looks at Keely, his voice slow and even, thinking about the words as he says them.

Keely stands over him. She doesn't know what to say. Her mouth is open a little. She cannot imagine our father doing it, but I can. The way I picture it, he is in his gray suit, leaning over the edge of the tiny boat as if he were getting sick. The *Oh-My* lettering disappears and surfaces. Then the boat tips. It is early morning, sunrise, a little light shines on the bare spot on the back of his head, makes it look rosy, almost red. He somersaults in. His heavy black polished shoes take him down like two weights. He doesn't thrash or try to swim, just sinks, with his arms over his head and his lips pressed in a thin angry line. He would not be happy to die. He would feel it necessary, a duty, his face like a person's in a movie, positioned before a firing squad, terrified, resolute.

Derby sits quietly. Keely is still standing. She starts pacing up and down the dock.

"Why would he do it?" he asks, finally.

Keely stares blankly at me, then at Derby.

"He polished his shoes," I say. "I smelled that black Kiwi polish in the kitchen when I got home." I don't tell them where I had been—out with Quinn Porter, who brought us Irish soda bread from his mother, who drove to work in the city with our father, black-haired, smelling of lime, who unlaced my tennis shoes, pulling the string through every eyelet, saying, "I used to dress you when you were little," then kissing my toes, the arches of my feet, laughing softly, in the dark cellar of his mother's house.

"Maybe there was someone else," Keely says. "Maybe they went to Tahiti together."

"What was he like?" Derby L. stretches his foot out and places the sole of his boot against my foot. He stares at me with his red-rimmed eyes.

"He was someone who would never go to Tahiti," I say, calmly. I don't know this for sure. I think of the photograph of him and our mother here at George's house. They are much younger, sitting on the end of our dead grandmother's couch. He is grinning, leaning toward her, and she is leaning away, holding his hands back, clasping them at the wrist. The knuckles of her hands are white, her lips are dark, open, laughing. It is a group picture. Everyone else is quietly posing. "We ruined the picture," she once said, shaking her head, but smiling a little. I never saw them that way. They always moved around each other, never touching, and I wonder how things must pass so easily in and out of our memories, how I can know exactly the shape of Quinn Porter's mouth, the taste of the chain where his St. Francis medal hung, and the smell of the room, like apples fermenting in the damp spaces behind the furnace, yet not know the sound of my father's voice, its tone, the depth of it bellowing across our yard, speaking within a room, or whispering at night behind a door.

I cannot waver from my story. Even the lake pulls me, its black depths cold now in the beginning of spring. I think if I dip my foot in it I will feel him in the water, flowing in the currents, swirling around my ankle.

"He wasn't a good person," I say. "He shouldn't have left us, either way."

"He brought us pastries every Sunday. He had a big smile," Keely says.

"He never smiled," I tell Derby L. "He did bring us pastries, though. He drank whiskey at night by himself." The pastries came on Sundays, from the Italian bakery, napoleons and éclairs and berry tarts. We sat around the kitchen table and drank Constant Comment tea and he would wink at me, crumbs covering the white crisp front of his shirt, his hair wet, combed back, the lines of the comb etched into the ridge of hair over his forehead. I stare at this in my mind and it is like a framed picture, as if all the scenes of our lives were just this one. I can examine details—the shape of sun on the wooden floor, the gauzy curtains, mid-flap, my mother's hair colored near-red, the bend of her body, her outstretched arm, and the frozen wink of my father's eye that is like a pain in my mind, that makes me so achingly happy I feel the need to cry.

"Am I here to figure all this out?" Derby L. asks. I can't tell if he is irritated or joking. He rubs his hands over his eyes, puffs air into his cheeks, then lets it out.

"There's nothing to figure out," I laugh.

"Just you," he whispers, with his hand cupped around his mouth, like a secret. He watches me, a little sadly, and I am nervous about the look in his face, the way his eyes settle on me. I close my eyes and listen to the gentle slap of the lake under the dock. I imagine my husband asleep on the couch, snoring, ignorant, his thick arms thrown back over his head. I married him too young. Had my father been not-gone he would have objected, forbidden it, and knowing this I defied him, in exhilaration, half-expecting him to appear out of nowhere and say something. My husband is a grinning, gentle man. He doesn't like to come here. He is nervous around my mother. She stares at him without recognition, or she feeds him piles of food on Lenox china and hovers, calling him Edward, my father's name. My husband and I have new friends in a new town. He believes I am happy, but he knows nothing about me. He doesn't even know that he doesn't love me.

When George's green International pulls in, we are lying flat with our backs pressed against the weathered slats of the dock, staring straight up at Derby L.'s constellations. He points them out to us, though I am sure he is too drunk to see anything. His voice trembles a little.

George stands at the end of the dock like a ghost. I can see, in the dark, how different he is, fuller, broader, his arms dangling the same, but heavier. For a second I am afraid to say anything. George swings an arm and says, "Come on," in a voice I don't recognize. Derby L. gets up first, and Keely and I follow them through the back door into the kitchen.

Inside, the house hasn't changed. I know where to look to find the ancient spices on their rack, the calendar, the kitchen clock. I know what is in each drawer. I am sure it is the same with the other houses along the lake. No one redecorates. Things collect, they are never thrown away. And so I see, immediately, the old family photograph propped in front of the stack of *National Geographics*, next to the ceramic ashtray shaped like a fish.

Keely and George go to find sleeping bags and Derby L. flops down on the couch and kicks off his giant boots. I think he will pass out, but he waits until we spread the sleeping bags on the carpeted floor. George turns out the lights before we are all settled. I hear him grope his way down the hall and fumble with his bedroom door. I am sure that Derby L. will lie down next to Keely, but somehow I am stuck in the middle between them.

"Do you want me to move?" I ask Keely. She grabs my arm and hisses, "No," and I wait for Derby L. to say, "I heard that," but he doesn't. He wheezes a few feet away. From his room I hear George's belt buckle clank against the iron bedrail. Keely sleeps curled next to me with her head near my shoulder. The dark turns gray and I make out the shapes in the room, Derby's boots leaning against each other, a vase of fake gladiolas, and the photograph, its black-and-whiteness shimmering at me from the shelf. Derby L.'s arm is against mine. I feel him take my hand. He holds it carefully as if it might fall apart in his, then traces it, up and down each finger, like a pattern on my skin I'm supposed to remember.

In the morning, half-awake, I mistake the warmth of my sister's body for that of my husband's, and I think I am in my house in our big brass bed. If I open my eyes I will see his leg lying on top of the white sheet, the open window across the room, and outside, our apple tree light green, growing, and the ground under it, covered with white blossoms, looking like snow. Instead I hear an engine running and I open my eyes to another room, dim, airless, and my sister curled like a child sleeping beside me.

Outside, George and Derby L. have the boat out. Derby wears a pair of George's cut-off jeans. He is shirtless, and his back and legs are white as bones. He climbs into the boat and they head away from the dock before I can call to them. The water of the lake churns brownish-black by the motor, alive now, moving toward shore where it grabs the long grass, the marsh marigolds, and the brown sandy edges.

I open a few windows and pull back the drapes. Keely says something in her sleep. I search the dresser drawers in the back spare bedroom and find some more cut-offs and three old bathing suits, spares that we kept here, Keely, my mother, and I. They are long out of style. My mother's is navy blue, trimmed in white braid like rope, with an anchor sewn on one hip. The top is full of wire, so that when I hold it up the chest pokes out in front. These will still fit us, I think. The bathing suits smell like the pine wood of the dresser. They are faded and thin. I put mine on and stare at myself in the mirror. I imagine I will call my mother and she will stop by and put hers on, too. And then she will become a different person, move through her nephew's house like she used to, grabbing magazines off the table, swatting flies, her hair wrapped in a print scarf, her feet bare on the wood floor of the kitchen. She will laugh the kind of laugh that doubled her over, that made her body shake without sound.

I smile at myself because in the bathing suit I am seven years younger and I am sure then, in the gray light of the spare room, there is no such thing as time. I can open any door and he will be sitting by the window reading, the wind blowing the pages of the book, his thumb holding the pages down. I will tiptoe around him, not daring to approach him. I imagine my mother might do the same in our old house, walk into the bedroom and see a quilt bunched on the side of a bed, see how it resembles him sleeping. And I wonder if she continues past the room, pretends for the rest of the day that it is him—speaking to him through the doorway, kneading the dish towel, cooking his food again, not making the bed at all, keeping it that way for longer than a day, maybe even slipping in alongside him at night, cautiously, slowly, prolonging the moments until her arm thrown in sleep flattens the quilt. I cannot imagine what she feels then—loss, anguish, and something else, that urges her out into her garden, that lets her walk away, travel the neighborhood and return at night, or not return at all, to sleep, one summer night, in Mr. Leone's field, under a wide-branched elm.

I put my mother's suit away in the drawer and bring Keely hers. She holds it up to herself, her eyes blurred with sleep.

"Put it on," I say.

She stares at me and I model for her.

"It'll fit you," I tell her. She clutches the bathing suit to her chest and smiles, but I see she will not try it on. I dance around the room and jump onto the couch. Keely watches me. I hear the boat outside and I run out the back door and down the dock.

Derby L.'s hair has been blown straight back. George points at me and laughs.

"Where's your sister?" he asks. He jumps onto the dock and Derby L. is at the wheel.

"Get in," he says. "Let's go."

The lake water foams white. The motor is a soft, low mumble. George holds the edge of the boat so I can climb over. My bare feet slip on the floor, wet with spray and ice cold. I cannot help but shiver, though the air isn't cold until we begin to move. I think I should have worn a shirt or something. I grab onto the back of one of the seats to keep from falling. When we reach the center of the lake, Derby L. cuts the engine and we idle there. It is windy on the lake and even though we are sitting still, my hair blows over my face and into my mouth.

Derby L. lifts his sunglasses. "Is this about the spot?" he asks.

I shield my eyes from the sun and look toward the shore. I see Keely on the dock. Her two arms wave in the air like matchsticks. George sits on the porch in a fluorescent chaise lounge. I wonder if Derby is trying to be malicious, bringing me out here. I stare at him and he stares back. He moves toward the side of the boat and leans over.

"I don't see anything," he says. "Do you want to swim?"

Probably, up on shore, my husband is calling George's house, trying to find me. Keely is wondering what I am doing, wearing my old bathing suit out in the middle of the lake with Derby L. The boat rocks back and forth. The sun warms me and I move up next to Derby and look over into the black water. He is right, there is nothing there, except his shadow and mine.

"We can't see the bottom," I say. I stay there, watching the water, searching for the place where my father's bones will glow white in the murk on the floor of the lake. I feel Derby L.'s arms around me, pulling me back. Now, my mother is out in her yard, tugging at weeds in her wild garden, stooping on hands and knees in the meadow grass that was once a lawn, her eyes unfocused, blue-gray, the color of the paint bubbling, peeling off the house behind her. My sister is on the phone in George's house, begging another boyfriend to pick her up, giving directions that he will not be able to follow, that will bring him to another town so much like this one he will not even know he is lost. He will pass the small white-washed store at the bottom of a hill lined with low walls that spill stones into the narrow road. He'll look for the lake and the cedar-shingled house, for Keely waiting out front, and see another girl instead, standing in a patch of bluets by a galvanized mailbox, its bright red flag up. She will wave him down, lean on the car door with one hip out, trick him into driving her somewhere, the name of a town she has heard of, the sound of the name the magical source of her desire—Coventry, Mystic, Darien.

George lounges on the porch peering at us through his binoculars. I am on the boat and I cannot escape. Derby L. holds me around the waist. I think of my father in the little boat and he is not ready to jump, he is rowing, wearing green swim trunks and I am in the prow, fishing with a drop line. He dips an oar, splatters me with water and I am soaked, giggling, seven or eight years old in a bright pink bikini. I am startled by this memory. I did not will or invent it, it appears on its own, authentic.

There was no body. There are no bones. I am under the lake's spell, pulled down into the greenish-black, lulled by the watery slap against the bottom of the boat.

"I want to go back," I say. I want to go back to our house and bang in the breezeway door and feel the coolness of the beige linoleum squares, listen to the wind chimes, aqua fish tinkling like glass. I will go into their room and slide the closet door and smell my father's clothes, hide in them, shut the door behind me, step into his leather shoes, and brush the dust from the tops. In the bureau drawers I will find small bottles of saccharine, golf tees, socks in balls, blue, brown, and green, a picture I drew of Keely and me, standing around a Christmas tree in triangle bodies. And I will smell the old brown pennies in their cardboard box, pick them up, hold them in my hand, until the damp tight part of my hand smells just like them.

"And anyway," I say, "it's cold."

"But that's why I'm here," says Derby L.

I look at his face and wonder where his glasses have gone. His eyes look back at me, bare, swollen pink underneath. He laughs and so do I. He reels me in closer to him, and it is not such a bad place to be. The boat rocks us back and forth, and we dance a little, to keep our balance. I don't think of anything. It is peaceful, not thinking. I do the dance and stay close. Somehow everything moves where it belongs—his arms, my hands, everything fits into place, even the past falls back.

"And so—" he says, into my hair.

But the water said it first, small sounds against the boat, rhythmic, like music that Derby has given words to and spoken. My memory swoops through years and days to get here. I whirl with it and see the space between Quinn Porter's eyes where his eyebrows met, hear the sound of my husband's laughing with my head pressed against his chest, then my father's breath against my ear, smelling of whiskey and coffee, whispering, "Goodnight," the sharp brush of his cheek against mine, and the green vines on the wallpaper climbing up, up.

My memory takes in everything, the smell of the lake, Derby L.'s face, his eyes half-closed against the pollen in the air, his nose running, his long dark whips of hair, wet, hanging. I take his hands from my waist. I hold them out by the wrist, and they flap in the air, fingers splayed. I do not want to give them back. I watch them struggle, pale white against blue sky, frail, quivering, like bird's wings.

Leaf House

The night after Martha's father died of a lightning strike on Penwood Pond, the sounds of crickets came from the foundation of the house, and fireflies pulsed, eerie and tender, at the edge of the woods. Martha left home and walked two miles to the center of town, past Filley Park and its shadows gathering like skirt folds, past the hardware store's smell of loam and chlorine, the Mobil station and its brilliant fluorescence, the library's brick façade where the gnarled roots of trees buckled the sidewalk. She crossed the town green, the grass cool and dewy, to the sidewalk that circled the new Wintonbury Mall, a maze of offices and shops with a fountain at its center. When Michael pulled into the parking lot she simply stepped off the curb and he stopped and she got in. She was sixteen. This is how she remembered it happening. It may have been that her skirt, a flimsy wraparound, had blown open as she stepped down off the curb, or there had been something slightly desperate about her smile, or the way she held her hands out in front of her. He may have had to step on the brakes to avoid hitting her, but she didn't recall hearing the squeal of tires, or feeling any threat of injury. She would attend her father's funeral at the Sacred Heart Church with her sorrow checked by the memory of what she'd done on the narrow seats of Michael's silver MG.

Michael was an older boy. He already had a girlfriend, one he took out to restaurants in neighboring towns, places like Pettibone's Tavern or Avon Old Farms Inn where Martha had gone as a child. He told Martha they sat in booths and talked, or in his car parked out under the stars and talked, and he claimed she let him kiss her, but nothing more went on. At the time, it had been easy for Martha to pretend this girlfriend meant nothing to him. When she was with him he looked at her with such longing, his eyes so intensely blue they took on a shade of misery she still saw years later as his wife, fixing him a vodka tonic at the kitchen counter, turning to glance at him sitting with his head in his hands at the kitchen table. Overhead, the globe-shaped light gave the room a bluish tint, and beyond the large picture window the backyard woods were in darkness. Michael and Martha had two daughters, and virtually no memories of the past to interrupt their lives.

Their house, in a new suburb in rural Connecticut, was a white Dutch Colonial with a red door, and an expansive lawn that sloped up to the street. When Martha and Michael had first driven down Maple Hill Drive, they'd seen children on bicycles and husbands watering flowerbeds. The tree boughs had swayed overhead, and Martha thought she heard the chimes of the ice cream truck. They bought the house that summer, despite Michael's insistence that they couldn't afford it, because Martha knew in her heart that it was their destiny to live there. "I have a feeling," she kept saying.

"It's only a house," Michael told her.

"It will be our lives," Martha said.

She spoke fervently, her eyes swimming. She would win him, aware that each time she did there would be a price exacted, as if a bargain had taken place. The conditions were never spoken, but she believed he kept a kind of tally, that one day she would owe him for the privilege of having her way. This kept her wary of his moods, and just this summer, one year after their move, she could see that perhaps a balancing of the account would be his falling out of love with her.

She had sensed it first in May, when the lawn became a bright, almost false green. The bulbs she had planted came up, and in the mulched beds around the house, plants emerged and opened and bloomed and Martha went out onto the back porch in the mornings and breathed in and felt part of whatever was happening around her in the woods. Michael shut himself off, preferring to sit in the dark kitchen bent over his coffee and toast, the burden of the mortgage rounding his shoulders. One morning when she urged him to step outside and look at the backyard, the apple trees suddenly, completely in bloom, he shook his head, and when she tried to grab his arm, to pull him out, he shrugged her off, and she saw that it wasn't the morning or spring that he didn't want, it was her.

Wallis and Lucie came downstairs into the kitchen, their faces closed off as if they sensed something charged in the room. They took out their tiny colored cereal bowls and each got spoons. Wallis went into the pantry and brought out the cereal, silent and purposeful, like her father. Lucie was eight years old, the youngest, the more animated, dark-haired and tiny. Wallis was ten, and she had started to lengthen and thin and become almost sallow. She wanted her blond hair long, to her waist—an unflattering length. She reminded Martha of a child from another era, one who wore cumbersome skirts and bonnets and shoes she had to labor over with a buttonhook. Martha realized she had grouped the four of them—that she believed Lucie was like her, and Wallis like Michael, that Wallis and Michael were the stolid, serious ones, the martyrs, and she hated this about them. Wallis poured the cereal into the bowls on the table, and her face pinched with exactness. Martha watched her from the doorway to the den where Michael had retreated with his paper. Before he left he would enter the kitchen to kiss both girls good-bye, and look at her as he did this, a look that Martha always interpreted as "These are ours, these beautiful girls," but that today she sensed meant something else, a kind of vindication: "These are mine, and don't you forget it."

She imagined an alliance had been formed—surreptitiously, between the three of them. Their faces touched, their arms intertwined, and Martha waited by the doorway for her little kiss, a small, dry press of lips on hers. Any other day she did not care, but on this morning, the one of the apple blossoms, the lifeless kiss drained her and left a spark of anxiety that grew as summer approached and the girls' school ended. As she cleaned and scoured and scrubbed, furiously, hoping to douse it. As the humidity of summer took over, and the mornings were full of cicada noise, and inside, the house fell more and more silent.

Once summer vacation began, the girls moved outdoors with packs of children that showed up at the house each morning. Martha didn't need to get out of bed to know what they were doing, or who was there, tapping at the screen door. Wallis would send Lucie up to tell her they were going down the street, to the Sheas', or the Langs', or out into the backyard. Two hours earlier Michael would have gotten up and showered and slathered on the lime-scented aftershave he got each year on Father's Day, put on his clothes, and left for work. Of this, she remembered only the weight of him on the edge of the mattress, slipping on his socks. The mornings could operate with ease, without her moving from under the cool bed sheet.

During the day the neighborhood women gathered in small groups to sip iced coffees and watch toddlers in plastic pools. They wore cotton shells and twill shorts and sandals decorated with sequins and shells and colored rhinestones, like a school craft project. They were women her age, some younger, who had set aside plans to go to law school, or medical school, given up positions as financial planners, bankers, and account executives. When Martha was a girl, she was one of them. They were there at summer camp, forming friendships in cabins and on the brown sand beaches of Lake Champlain. She knew them from her private school, where they wrote their names in big, chunky letters on the covers of their binders and wore clogs and chinos and turtlenecks. They summered at Point O'Woods, in Maine, or on the Vineyard, boated the Connecticut River to Hamburg Cove. In the winter months they went to Florida or the Virgin Islands. All of this before her father died.

Now Martha was part of their circle again, while Lucie splashed with a friend in one of their pools and Wallis arranged games on the wide lawn. She knew how to ask the right questions to get them all talking so that she could relax back into a folding chair and listen to the drone of their voices. They were Missy, and Grace Perry, girls who went to Smith and Mount Holyoke, who shared a camaraderie that kept Martha at a distance. There were stories of late-night sorority parties, and mutual friends from a world Martha never had a chance to enter. They discussed difficulties with babies and toddlers that Martha had never experienced, so that even in the raising of her children she was a stranger. None discussed a husband who had fallen out of love.

Later, they took the children in for lunch served on paper plates and watched the soap operas while the little ones napped. The street was quiet under its tree bough canopy, the leaves shifting, making shushing noises. Martha enjoyed the flow of the women in and out of houses, the children's sounds of play, the absence of husbands and their heavy footfalls, demanding things in kitchens. Each day was tirelessly similar, and in their sameness, Martha forgot her dissolving marriage.

In June there was an emergency on Foothills Way, the street behind them, and everyone on Maple Hill came out of their houses when the fire rescue truck passed. It was just after dinner, and the children jumped on their bikes to find out what had happened, riding off into the dusk and disappearing. The adults waited near the ends of their driveways for the news that filtered down the street from CeCe Lang, who had actually walked around the block to witness the tragedy—a little girl had drowned in a shallow brook that ran behind the houses on Michael and

Martha's side of the street. She had fallen and hit her head. The children pedaled back, pale, uncomprehending. The tones of the parents became hushed. The wives put their hands to their mouths, the husbands placed arms over their wives' shoulders. All of this while the moths emerged to beat at the porch lights, and the neighbors gathered into small, awed groups. No one really knew the child. She had been born with Down syndrome, someone said. She had been from the street over, and their little groups around the pools hadn't included anyone from Foothills.

Martha stood beside Michael and held her own girls' hands, watched the people leave their driveways and lawns and congregate. She followed him as he moved down the street, and found herself in a small group of neighbors she did not know. They were older, in their forties, Martha guessed, and one of the women was smoking a cigarette, blowing the smoke up into the night sky where it formed a little cloud above their heads. They were talking about another time—years before, when this same thing had happened. "You'd think they'd fill that brook in, or something," the woman with the cigarette said. The girls tugged on Martha's hands, and the woman smiled at them, then turned to Martha. "Oh, let them go," she said. Her voice was a little hoarse, but pleasant, a laughing voice. "They're all playing hide-and-seek." And she pointed to the yard behind her, where a large group of children were scattering, their bodies flashes of light-colored clothing and skin. Martha grudgingly let go of their hands, and her palms were wet from gripping them. One of the men had left the group and returned with bottles of beer, and the woman placed one in Martha's hand, patting it in a motherly way. "I know it's an awful thing, Martha," she said.

Martha looked at her, surprised. The woman smiled and Martha could see fine wrinkles around her eyes and mouth. "I'm Helen," she said, "Of Helen and Steve. We've heard all about you from Michael. I was just telling him the other day we needed to get together, the four of us. Finally welcome you to the neighborhood." Around them the men's voices became boisterous. They laughed and slapped each other's backs and lit up cigarettes, and forgot the drowned girl. Martha saw Michael accept a cigarette, watched one of the older men lean over with his lighter. In the light from the flame, Michael's face looked childish to Martha. He had never mentioned any of these people, but Martha remembered times she would look out and see the rake propped against the maple tree in front, or the mower in the driveway covered with cut grass, and Michael nowhere in sight. And she realized he had been with these neighbors—in their garages or their kitchens, sipping cold beers and lighting cigarettes, talking about her. He had gone off and she hadn't bothered to ask him where, as if it had been of no importance. She had wanted him to have friends in the neighborhood, but she had not suspected they would be like these—settled and jaded, women like Helen Halsey, who wore the evidence of her affairs like wampum, who kept her hands on Michael as if he were a prize.

Michael had grown up in a large brick house with two life-sized stone deer flanking the front door. Behind his house was a swimming pool surrounded by a wooden deck, and a boathouse on a pond whose tributaries fed into the very pond, a mile away, where Martha's father had died. Martha had known all of this about him before she stepped off the curb in front of his MG that night. She had gone to his house one winter with a friend to ice skate. There had been a three-sided shelter built on the banks of the frozen pond, with a fire burning and benches to sit on, and she had come in off the ice and watched him from across the room, his breath making a white cloud around his head. Martha's friend had placed a gloved hand to Martha's ear and whispered his name, her breath smelling of spearmint schnapps. The shelter had been warm from the fire, and Michael had unwound his scarf, and his face had flushed from the heat. Martha could not pinpoint exactly what drew her to him. He had worn a knit hat and sat quiet and thoughtful in the midst of his loud, drunken friends, and maybe it was his composure, his self-assurance, that she liked. Later, when she'd gotten a closer look at him, it was his eyes, the blue of them below his blond hair, and though she had watched him all night, waiting for him to notice her, for a word or a moment with him, his eyes never lit on her, only passed her over, scanning the room for someone else. And because he never approached her, she never forgot him, kept imagining the idea of being with him on still summer evenings with her face pressed against the pillow, and the neighborhood sounds coming through her open window—boys out on front lawns playing lacrosse, husbands and wives walking dogs—or during the bus rides to the public high school, the town passing beyond the dirty bus window, knowing that one day she would have her chance. She has never told him this, not wanting their meeting to ever seem anything other than a work of fate.

Martha had always believed she could have whatever she wanted, even after her father died, and her mother started selling things from their house in her antique shop—the watercolors of ducks in flight, the Staffordshire spaniel that held open the door to the den, these things disappearing without a word, as if Martha and her brother weren't supposed to notice, and so they pretended they didn't—Martha's brother busy making a hideout in the basement, setting up a game of Monopoly and playing it by himself. And then the crying came at night from her mother's room, and Martha imagined everyone—the Crofts and the Deerfields taking out their trash, or searching in the shrubs for a lost cat—could hear her. Martha's life changed, but she did not accept any of it. Inside, she desired the same things, and it did not matter how she lived, what school she went to, what clothes she wore. She thought now, in the group of gathered neighbors, the grass damp and cool through her sandals, the night full of children's voices and deeper, adult laughter, that she had managed to save herself by never acknowledging the sense of loss that drew down the corners of her mother's mouth.

Beside her, Helen leaned conspiratorially, making plans for that Saturday evening—dinner somewhere, cocktails at seven o'clock. Behind them the children shrieked in the yard, overtired, and the other groups of neighbors moved inside and turned on their living room lamps and bedroom lights and called their own children indoors. Martha discovered Wallis and Lucie at her side and saw that the men had brought a galvanized tub of ice out to the circle where they stood, and Steve had brought folding chairs, and they continued to drink and laugh, the lit ends of their cigarettes marking their spots in the circle on Helen and Steve's front lawn.

Martha looked toward Michael, but he had settled himself in a chair, his beer bottle nestled in the palms of his hands, and when she told him she should take the girls home he had leaned toward her, his head cocked, distracted. Helen patted his knee and he turned back toward the conversation on his left, so Martha and the girls were forgotten, except for a dismissive wave of his hand. She waited a moment, listening to Steve tell the story of the last time a child had drowned in the brook—the Martin boy, or the Piteks', wasn't it? he said. And then how they had all gone over to George Deason's place, and the kids had all fallen asleep on the rec room shag, and George's wife, Mary Gail, had made pancakes at four a.m. Helen tipped her head back and laughed and slapped her leg. "And remember one batch caught fire?" she said. Martha had never met the people they were talking about, though their daughter had been her babysitter for months.

"That was a long time ago," Steve said. He shook his head, and the group grew quiet, as if observing a moment of silence. Martha wondered what had happened to the family to cause such a pall. Someone cast a quick look over their shoulder at the Deasons' house—and then Helen reminded them of the whiskey sour tasting party, and the lobster bake, and how they steamed the lobsters, twenty or thirty of them, over an open pit dug right into the lawn, and fueled by a mixture of charcoal briquettes, lighter fluid, and firewood left from winter.

"And Barrows headed up the street singing," Steve said. Someone lit a cigarette. Martha saw Michael edge forward in his chair, his shoulders hunched away from her, listening.

She rose and gathered the girls and walked back up the street to their house, which sat dark and open at the top of the hill. Inside, it was airless and hot and smelled of the meal she had cooked and hadn't cleaned up—the ragged chicken bones still on the broiler pan on the stove, the plates still spread on the kitchen table by the bay window. Lucie wanted to watch television, but it was too late for that, and Martha knew that she would have to read her a book to get her settled, maybe even lie beside her in her small bed until she fell asleep, and she resented all of this, pining for the circle of adults down the street, the sound of their conversation, the cold beer bottle with its label sliding off in her hand.

Wallis would not sleep in her room. She stood, in her nightgown with her arms crossed, at the threshold of Lucie's room, and so the three of them lay down in Martha and Michael's bed, and Martha read a few pages of *The Secret Garden* until both girls were asleep. She stayed there in the bed, listening for the neighbors down the street, imagining them in their circle—Steve and Howard Livesy in their polo shirts, their stomachs rounding over their waistbands, and Howard's wife, Marilyn, with her jangling bracelets, her tiny upper lip that revealed her gum line; Jodie and Seth, a young couple with a live-in nanny, who could stay out of the house as long as they liked; and Helen beside Michael, her hand on his leg, her nails exquisite and opalescent, her eyes and voice laughing. Once, Martha imagined, she had worn Pappagallo flats with the flowers on the toes, and sundresses that revealed her fragile shoulder blades. Martha tried to remember what Michael had been doing in the group, other than smiling his usual grin, his head bobbing in agreement. She imagined him returning Helen's glances, placing his own hand on her bare knee, and she felt a spiraling emptiness. Outside, beyond the cricket and the frog sound, a laugh rang out, tinny and distant, and downstairs the plates with their remains marked their places at the table.

Martha closed her eyes and dreamed, not of Michael and Helen, but of the little drowned girl she did not know. Her body was small and sturdy. She wore a dress covered with tiny lady-bugs. Her hair curled over her ears, and she walked, barefoot, to the edge of the brook. The stones, covered with green algae, made a slippery path across to the other side and a sandy bank. Brook water trickled over the green tops—innocent, clear, its depths filled with frogs and small fish. And before the girl stepped onto the first stone, her arms held out to balance, Martha reached down and touched the skin of her arms and her face, smelled the laundry soap on her clothes and the sweat in her hair. She breathed the girl in and knew the scent of her mother's perfume caught in the dress's folds. Martha awoke with her face pressed to Lucie's neck, but it would take moments, still lost in the clarity of the dream, to realize she had been breathing in the smells of her own child.

She cleared the table at one a.m., and when Michael came in she was at the sink, scrubbing the broiler pan and crying. She had wanted Michael to see her, to step behind her and ask her why, so she could tell him that they were all self-involved and petty, that a real little girl who had lived a street away had died in the small, half-dried-up brook that ran behind their house, and none of them cared. She had wanted him to take her soapy hands in his and hold her so she could smell his lime cologne and the beer and the smoke from their neighbors' cigarettes. But he had not walked past the kitchen, had gone upstairs instead, his footfalls on each carpeted step a slow shuffle, and she was left crying at the sink for a girl she did not know, for someone else's tragedy.

Through Martha's kitchen bay window she could see through the trees to the outlines of the houses on Foothills. One after-noon someone played a piano, and the music, a slow sarabande, drifted through the gnarled apple boughs and pine branches heavy with sap and needles, across the small brook, into their backyard. Martha was in the kitchen making potato salad, and the sound came through the window screens. She stopped what she was doing, left the potatoes steaming in a bowl, and went out the back onto the deck, and then down through their patch of woods to the tangled underbrush that led to the brook. She saw that her own children had worn a path through the ferns and skunk cabbage and thorn bushes, the spindly jack-in-the-pulpit, and she took it, through shoulder-high grasses to a cleared area by the bank. It was hot and humid, and mosquitoes and dragonflies whirred down from the tops of trees. The music had stopped, and she stared at the small flow of water, the way it coursed through a narrow gully. It ran over large rocks and brownish leaves and debris caught in small eddies. And out of nowhere, a man appeared. He stood farther down the bank, on the opposite side, wearing slacks and a wrinkled dress shirt. He had his tie loosened, and his leather shoes were planted in the dirt. Martha saw him glance up at her. His eyes reached hers across the trickle of the brook, in the haze and the whine of cicadas. She stared at the base of his throat where the loosened tie and his collar met.

"Was that you?" she said. "Playing?"

He shook his head no. She saw his hand go to the tie as if to straighten it. And then the music started up again, and Martha imagined one of those lonely boys with odd haircuts you'd see in the halls at school—strange and distant, with hidden musical gifts. The piece, a scherzo, went on for several bars and then stopped. They listened then to the sound of the brook, waiting, but the music didn't resume. The man said he had played once as a child, and Martha too told how she was forced to practice with a metronome.

"In the summer it got hot, and my legs stuck to the bench and that ticking went on and on."

The man smiled at her, nodding. "Did you study privately?"

"With our neighbor Mrs. Tipton," Martha said.

"*The* Mrs. Tipton? On Sharon Road?"

Martha smiled, amazed. They were both from the same town. They'd gone to the same high school.

"The fighting War Hawks," he said, laughing, his head thrown back in a way that Martha found winning.

They'd graduated many years apart. The man was older, his hair graying. Martha told him she wouldn't have guessed. He smiled and shook his head. "You say that to every man you meet in the woods," he said. They laughed. Around them the trees stilled. Martha said how sad it was about the little girl. She went on, as she often did when she was nervous, about how awful it must be to lose a child, how she didn't know what she'd do if it had been one of her own. The man made a coughing sound into his hand and she looked up to see his blanched face. He glanced away, as if something had flitted off into the trees. It occurred to her that the little girl might have been his. "Oh," she said. The man kept his pained expression averted. It was as if neither of them knew how to disentangle themselves from the idea of it, thrown out now into the air between them. Martha felt the urge to take his face in her hands.

"I'm so sorry." She took a step forward, treading on the jack-in-the-pulpit. "If there's anything I can do," she said.

He looked at her, steadily, and shook his head. "Why don't you come up?" He gestured with his hand up through the woods to what she presumed was his house.

Martha did not know if she should.

"I'd like the company," he said. His face was mapped with an uncomfortable sadness. Martha smiled, wanly, sorry for him. She slipped off her shoes, and like the girl in her dream, she stepped across the wide stones to the opposite bank. The girl's father gently took her elbow in his hand.

"Richard," he said. His hand slipped into hers, soft and assured.

Martha said very little of what she was thinking. She followed him, dumbly, through the saplings and fern, up an incline that had no path. Richard seemed to chart his own, holding back thorny tendrils of wild blackberry for her to pass. She thought, "It is almost time for lunch," and "The girls will wonder where I've gone." She imagined she heard the phone ringing in her house behind her, or Wallis's voice calling out. She wondered what his wife would think about her showing up. She followed along behind Richard until they came out into an expanse of lawn, green and tended and bordered by the wild lilies that bloomed on the roadsides, *shithouse lilies,* her father called them, and she almost said this out loud to Richard as she stepped up alongside him. The house was a modern design, made of cedar siding and one long wall of glass. They stood there on the lawn, looking up at it.

Martha made a sound of appreciation. "It's lovely."

There was a porch, similar to Martha's, and they climbed this set of steps up, and Richard opened the sliding screen door for Martha to pass into the house. All this time he'd been talking about his work. He was an attorney with a large firm downtown. They stepped into the kitchen where one lone bowl sat in a stainless sink, the sink wide and deep, like a tub. The cabinets were pale wood, with chrome pulls, the appliances all stainless. On the stone counter was a beautiful blue glass pitcher. The light fell into the shape of tree boughs on the floor. Martha saw the dim rooms opening off the nearby hallway—one side of the house in light, the other shadow. She couldn't imagine a child living here.

"All this silence gets to me," he said, his voice low.

He went to the refrigerator and took out a bottle of white wine. "Will you join me?" he asked her. "I don't want to drink alone."

Martha stayed by the sliding door. She could hear the leaves moving, and she glanced behind her. A bit of her house's roof was visible. "I don't know," she said.

Richard didn't seem sure if she understood his question. He waited with the wine bottle sweating in his hand. His eyes implored her to be accommodating. "Don't give me any grief," her mother used to say to her. Martha shook her head. She opened her mouth to protest, and he took down two glasses. The house seemed empty, and she wondered if his wife worked, or had gone to stay elsewhere—with a mother or a sister. He kept his eyes on her, as if she might bolt. He was kind, and careful, shaking his head.

"I know what you must think," he said, his voice barely audible. He slid the glass of wine across the counter.

Martha wanted to ask him what that was. "My girls might be coming home for lunch," she said. And then she wondered if that was the wrong thing.

"Just one drink," was all he said back.

He reached up into another cabinet and took down a bottle of scotch and poured himself a glass. Martha took the wine. She moved with it into the adjoining room and then stepped further into the house—the windows at the front were high and narrow, with slatted wooden blinds closed against the street. The room was sparely decorated—a long, pale couch, a glass table. There were smudges on the table, a teacup, a plate littered with greasy crumbs, an old sweater draped over the couch back, newspapers stacked messily on the cushions. She saw a pair of women's shoes by the front door. There were photographs that she did not approach. Martha heard children passing on Foothills Way, imagined them on their bikes, pedaling slowly, discussing what to do, pointing out the house where the drowned girl lived. Their voices rose, sharp and high-pitched. Behind her she heard Richard's intake of breath. She felt his hand on her shoulder. She put the glass of wine to her lips and drank.

"It must be very difficult for your wife." Martha kept her voice low to match the hush of the room. "All of the memories here." She thought he would tell her where his wife was now that she'd mentioned her, but he did not. His eyes were dark and concentrating on her face. He gave her a wry smile and took her free hand and brought it to his lips. Martha started, and spilled her wine on the carpet. He took her glass from her then and pulled her up against him and leaned his forehead down to touch her shoulder. She thought she should wipe the wine up off the rug, but he held her there, his mouth pressed to her collarbone. He smelled of pine woods. He whispered her name.

"Oh, Richard," she said. She expected at any moment that he would pull away, and apologize. And yet he did not. The moment, prolonged, could no longer be explained. He made a small sound, like a moan. Martha's clothing felt sodden and heavy from the heat in the room. Something stirred in her, stealthily, like a warm confusion. Richard moved the flat of his hand to her stomach. She let him do this because she found she wanted him to. His fingers slid up beneath her shirt, and then down under the waistband of her shorts. In a moment they had undone the clasp. She tipped her face up, opened her mouth onto his. She could no longer be accountable for where his hands went, or what they did. She leaned into the length of him. The room filled with the sudden, startling whir of cicadas.

At first, she felt observed by people who could not possibly see her—her mother, Michael, the missing wife, the boy playing the piano, the little drowned girl's ghost. When she made a sound, Richard said, "Shhh," as you might to a child who needed consoling. He brushed the newspapers to the floor, urgently. The couch's upholstery stuck to her skin. Like the piano bench, she thought. So little had passed between them she could think of nothing else. The sweater on the sofa arm smelled of a woman's perfume. Above her Richard's soft, graying hair stood on end. His forehead shone. His face was closed, and intent, an almost agonized expression. From somewhere upstairs came the sound of a door opening, and footsteps, another door closing. His eyes opened, and Martha saw the panic in them. He moved off of her, and pulled her up from the couch.

"I'm sorry," he said. "But you'll have to go."

He fumbled with his pants, with his shirt buttons. Martha tugged on her shorts. She saw they'd left a damp spot on the couch.

Martha had crossed the brook and reached the woods, and in her hurry to flee she'd taken another path by mistake. This one brought her to a clearing where her girls and the neighbor's children had been playing. They had piled the fallen leaves and pine needles into outlines of rooms connected by narrow paths. Martha paused here. Her shorts clung between her legs. Her heart raced. She imagined the children working together, gathering the piles of leaves, someone telling them where to place the outlines, what room was what, all of them moving busily about the woods with their tasks. Like little bees, Martha thought. She followed one path that led to a large, flat rock. Nearby was a pile of decaying logs, and a pot balanced on top—a piece of her Farberware. A spoon stood inside it, and a stew of torn pokeweed leaves and berries floating in water they may have carried from the brook. Around the flat rock were smaller ones—a table and chairs. The kitchen, she thought. From here she could not see her own house, or Richard's. The brook tumbled past sun-warmed stones. Light filtered through the trees onto the waving fern.

She took another path and came upon a makeshift tent. Martha's old chenille bedspread hung over a rope tied between two trees. It was anchored down on each corner by rocks. Airy fabric was draped at either end to enclose the tent, and Martha recognized the curtains that had decorated the living room when they'd moved in. She'd put them in the basement in a box, too nice to throw out. Overhead the trees swayed, and the curtains on the tent moved out and back. The children had all gone home for lunch. Martha thought that her girls may have gone to a friend's house to eat. The other mother would ask about her, and Lucie would say they didn't know where she'd gone, and Wallis would give her a look. Martha remembered the potatoes on the counter. There was laundry, too, in a basket in the hallway. She stepped closer to the tent and parted the curtain door. Inside, a blanket covered the ground, and a book from the public library, *Gone-Away Lake*, was propped beside a small basket filled with swatches of fabric, thread, colored yarn, and buttons in a small baby-food jar. Martha crawled in and sat down in the tent. The bedspread was stippled with leaf shadow. The wind tugged and buckled the sides. She smelled dirt and the dried leaves.

That first night with Michael, when Martha had been sixteen, she had believed that there was nothing for her in the world. She considered now how it might have been any boy who pulled into the Wintonbury Mall parking lot and won her heart, and this no longer worried her. Martha lay back in the tent and knew she was not destined to be with Michael, even as she remembered first seeing his silver MG, the shine of it in the lot lights, the way it curved around and came within inches of her outstretched hands. The top was down and his hair was tousled, and he had grinned at her through the windshield. He had asked her if she needed a ride, and she had lied and told him, "Yes," and gotten into the car, smelled the leather interior, fit her legs into the space beside him.

"Where are you going?" he asked, his hand on the gear shift smelling of cologne, his shirt sleeve rolled up along his arm, dressed for a date, which was obvious to Martha now, but at the time she thought everything was for her.

"I'm not really going anywhere," she told him, her skirt split open to the tops of her legs, her skin damp and shiny from the walk. By this time the car had moved forward to the street, was poised to turn onto the main road. She had not known how to sound—she had simply said the words, and he paused, fidgeted with the gearshift for a moment, the car rolling backward, then forward while he looked at her, and she, finally, looked at him, and without hesitation the gear caught and the car pulled out onto Tunxis Avenue heading north.

"Where would you like to go?" he asked quietly, almost shyly, his eyes fastened to the road ahead. The wind pulled at her hair and the car sped by the places she had just passed walking. She placed her hand on top of his on the gearshift. He glanced at her hand on his, but for the most part kept his eyes on the road, and Martha had the chance to look at him—his shaved cheeks, the way his hair blew in the wind and revealed the place below his ear that was childish and soft. At the next light, a deserted intersection that led into another town, she leaned over and kissed him there, and he turned his face so that her mouth found his, and though she could not see the blueness of his eyes she knew they were on her, studying her in the dark, and the car moved on, and she placed her hand on his leg, felt the weight of his thin summer trousers and the heat of his skin beneath them. He kissed her for a long time at the next stop sign, his fingers woven in her hair, cradling her head, his mouth gentle and persistent. He moved on when a car approached, driving faster on the tiny roads, charting a route that Martha would follow the next day in her mother's car, to a closed park in Granby, where they turned off the concrete lot onto a grass path and he parked the car, and they were enfolded in darkness.

Martha knew that they talked about themselves at some point, but she did not remember anything but the feeling of his hands, the night sounds drowned out by the sounds of his breathing, his soft groans. His body and its weight were all that mattered, the positioning in the narrow bucket seat, her hands on the small of his back, and the night air touching her exposed breasts, her shoulders and neck, its coolness moving up between the spread of her legs. He had put the seat all the way back. Somewhere a dog on its runner barked at headlights. Bats dropped from eaves and charted courses over lawns ribboned by mower's blades, their voices scraping like rusty pasture gates. She imagined her father casting his silly line from his rowboat, his box of new lures opened in the stern, his floppy hat, the way his sideburns grew bushy near his ears. Late summer lightning struck the rod on Duncaster Mill. The cows loose on the golf course lowered themselves to the green. Martha's mother set her rings in the crystal dish by the sink, and the air came in through the window, filled with ozone and clover. Over Michael's shoulder Martha saw the sky, brilliant with stars.

They would not plan dates after this. He would not call her and ask her to dinner, or a movie, or a party, and pick her up smelling of the same cologne, wearing a nice shirt. She would go back to high school and date other boys. She would walk to the mall with her friends, or drive her mother's car, and see Michael coming out of the package store wearing jeans and a T-shirt, heading out with his own friends. He'd stop on the sidewalk and stare at her, the friends calling to him from their car. Or she would see him dressed again for a date, driving through the mall parking lot, and he might catch sight of her and pull over to talk to her, to ask her how she was, what was she doing. At midnight her friends might tell her his little car was circling the mall lot, John Brown's restaurant, the bowling alley, Filley Park, looking for her. He would pull up beside her, and she would climb into his car, and they'd go to the parking lot at Connecticut General, to the reservoir, or the grass road at the park in Granby. He would always have a bottle of something in the car—brandy, or schnapps, or wine, and they would pull in somewhere and drink and have sex. From the beginning, Martha had given him everything he wanted, and she did not regret any of it, despite what people said about her. They did not know his desperation, his ragged breathing, the damp shine of his skin under the moon, or that she had wanted all of this, had planned it all, and in the end, gotten what she wanted. Michael was still the boy in the silver MG, his eyes the same, with the same lost look, and she would still give him anything, but somehow he could not remember what it was he ever wanted from her.

Around her the leaf house corridors fanned out, leading to

other rooms claimed by other children, decorated with rocks, and blankets and old sheets stolen from their mothers' linen closets, with discarded plates and cups, with tarnished cutlery and cracked vases filled with wood phlox. Martha remembered the drowned girl's father asking her to go. The way his hands hung loose, surrendered. He had made a terrible mistake. She saw his dismay that she had allowed him to do it, and yet she'd felt no remorse. Even now, lying on the blanket, the bedspread patterned with leaves overhead, her hands moved along her body in place of his. She'd left taking the porch steps quickly at his urging, crossing the lawn. At the entrance to the woods Martha had stopped and looked back. She hadn't expected to see him watching her, but there he'd been, raising his hand, a feeble farewell. She'd seen the glint of his watch. Then a woman had called to him from inside, and he'd turned, need driving him back into the house.

Mistresses

The day of the snowstorm, Ivy and Laurie shared a cigarette outside on the wall of the smoking pavilion at school. The sky was gray and geese flew overhead in their formation. It was late November, and the hickories and sycamores and maples had been stripped of their leaves, and the leaves had been blown to the curbs for the leaf collector, or raked and bagged, or, despite the town ordinance, burned in metal ash cans, fed to the bright flames by the armfuls. The sun rose over the dead grass and set behind the bare trees. Ivy felt that the only thing that could make this beautiful was snow, and that instinctively they were all waiting for it.

"Like you wait for your period," Laurie said gravely. She exhaled two perfect smoke rings. Her teeth were tiny and straight, like a child's.

Neither Laurie nor Ivy had been pregnant yet. But they knew what it was like to wait, stupidly, in those days when they allowed themselves to believe everything happened for a reason. They finished their cigarettes and rounded up Jonah and Billy and Marshall, tapping on the windows of their respective classes, signaling them to meet in the school parking lot. Billy Grant and Jonah Woodford were two boys Ivy and Laurie had chosen to be their boyfriends, though they didn't know who would end up with whom. Billy Grant's family, once soldiers who fought in the Battle of Bunker Hill, owned the local Hukelau restaurant. They also owned the strip mall with the bowling alley next door to the restaurant, and the land behind it that ran up to the cemetery. Some said they owned the cemetery itself, and so the bodies buried in it. There were also rumors they owned the rest of the dairy land that the Woodfords didn't. Billy and Jonah had been friends since their Congregational Church nursery school days. They'd both gone to the same private school and been kicked out for something they still hadn't divulged. Laurie and Marshall weren't the sort of people they normally hung around with. Marshall's father worked at the Grote and Weigel factory, inspecting casings for their famous hot dogs. Laurie's mother was a fixture of the Hukelau lounge happy hour.

Ivy's father worked, respectably, successfully, in insurance, but once he was called in for questioning concerning the suspicious death of the woman found at the bottom of the Connecticut River. Divers from a university environmental class discovered her the spring Ivy turned twelve. This was not something she could hide from in a small town. People always wanted to know if it was true the woman had bricks tied to her ankles, or if her feet weren't cemented into one of those galvanized tubs filled with ice and soda at annual Memorial Day picnics.

Even Jonah and Billy, once they made the connection, started with their own questions. They stood around Marshall's car in the parking lot, leaning on it, waiting for Marshall to show up. It was cold and they all wore sweatshirts, except for Billy, who had taken to wearing his grandfather's navy-issue peacoat—too big and smelling, faintly, of some lofty attic littered with insect wings. Jonah eyed him and stuck his hands in his sleeves. He did a little dance, hopping from one foot to the other, and stopped in front of Ivy.

"So," he said. "I heard that woman was nude."

Ivy smiled. "She had on one of those silk kimono-style robes and red patent-leather shoes," she told him. "She had long dark hair and it was tangled with seaweed."

Ivy had heard it all before. That the woman had been down there for years and was unrecognizable, or that she'd been there only a few months—her body caught youthful and supple in the divers' flashlights.

Marshall ambled down the grass hill to the lot, his body long and lanky and comical-looking. "What are we doing?" he asked.

"We're freezing," Billy said.

Jonah breathed out a white plume. "Unlock the car."

Ivy was never told how her father was connected to the crime. But it was easy enough to assume the woman had been his girl-friend, or at least that he'd slept with her at some point, maybe once or twice, or even regularly, that he'd left something of his at her apartment—one of her grandfather's monogrammed cuff links, a shirt that the dry cleaners had marked with his name. Ivy was sure there was plenty of physical evidence—hair and finger-prints, and body fluids—but not enough to arrest him, and no one else was ever accused. Her mother, a housewife who hadn't imagined any other sort of life, probably felt it wisest not to ques-tion his innocence. She never altered her usual activities, and Ivy's clothes still appeared freshly washed and folded at the end of her bed, and meals were prepared, and the rugs looked raked over by the vacuum, and the furniture still smelled of lemon polish every afternoon when Ivy got home from school. Maybe her mother wore a more fervent expression during Mass, and occasionally her face seemed puffy and pale, and the lines of the bedspread etched into her cheek revealed she'd been lying down in the middle of the day.

In the evenings before the woman was found there'd been phone calls, ones Ivy answered only to hear an extended silence on the other end. Sometimes there'd be the clink of glasses and a muffled din, what she'd later learn were sounds of a bar. Or she'd hear the Channel Three news, or the Boston Pops opening for *As Schools Match Wits*. She'd hear beyond these sounds to cars pass-ing on an interstate, doors opening and closing, and realize, when her first boyfriend plied her with screwdrivers and drove to the Berlin Turnpike one Saturday night, that the woman had called from a motel room. As a child, Ivy had waited, patiently listening on the stairs, the phone cord wrapped around the banister. She heard: *Keats wrote about this half-woman, half-serpent, believed by the Greeks to devour children. Once a beautiful woman loved by Zeus, she was punished by Hera in a jealous rage . . .* and then the buzzer, and a girl's voice, "Lamia." Ivy's house would smell of whatever had been prepared for dinner—standing rib roast or lamb chops, mashed potatoes, the oily smell of fish on Fridays. She listened to the sounds around her that must have filtered through the phone to the woman on the other end: the water running in the sink, the clank of china as her mother stacked the dirty plates, her mother's voice calling out to remind her of some chore she'd forgotten, or an appointment for the next day.

Ivy's mother thought the calls were for Ivy—one of her friends sharing a story about a girl they hated, the boy from math who, confusingly, pulled her chair out from under her, and then given her a cat pin with rhinestone eyes he'd found on the school blacktop. Eavesdropping, Ivy's mother discovered Ivy never made any response. She'd come out from the kitchen and stood over her with a dish towel.

"Who is it?" she'd asked.

D'Alembert's Trait de dynamique, *which declares the principle known by his name concerning the internal forces of inertia, was inferred from the laws of . . .* and a boy's voice cracking, "Newton." Sometimes, Ivy would hear a throat cleared on the other end, or a sigh, or a shifting. It was a woman, she'd determined. She'd hear her brush back long hair from the receiver. She'd hear her breaths in and out, raspy with a cold. She imagined her fanning wet nails, sitting on the side of a bed with her legs crossed, the smell of the polish thick in the room.

"I have to go now, Andrea," Ivy would say.

She still didn't know why she kept this up. The woman called, and both of them waited. She'd hear someone talking about the Hartford Whalers, the man's voice slurred, ice settling in a glass. Later, when the calls stopped and Ivy put the rumors and the phone calls together, she felt an incredible guilt. Maybe she had been the last person to share the woman's silence. Ivy accepted what she'd come to see as the potential truth in all of it. Her father, player of Heckedy Peg on lawns at dusk, swooping as a witch out of elm shadows to capture them, the man who, level-headed, pulled over to save a box turtle from certain death on Mills Pond Road, man of stories around summer fires, smelling of shaving soap, lime, tobacco, and Desenex foot powder, had been an adulterer. He sat in his den in his leather chair and never answered the telephone to learn his accomplice had wanted more from him. When Ivy grew old enough to want to disobey him, she did without any hesitation.

"I'm going out," she'd say. It would be evening, a school night, with a below-zero wind chill factor. Her father, forced to rise from his chair, folded his paper.

"You most certainly are not," he said.

Ivy paused at the door. "What are you going to do to stop me?"

Her father paled. "You're grounded, young lady," he said.

Ivy's mother stood behind him, biting her thumbnail. Ivy left the house anyway. She knew she had him, that there was nothing he could do to stop her, short of cementing her feet into a galvanized tub.

The day of the snowstorm Marshall pulled out of the school parking lot and turned onto Bloomfield Avenue. Ivy and Laurie sat up front with Marshall, and Billy and Jonah sat in the back. Their licenses had been revoked, and each of them had cars they were not allowed to drive. Billy's was in his garage, and Jonah's was out in his barn. Ivy and Laurie had never seen the cars, but they assumed they were sporty and new—convertible Firebirds, or Camaros, or something foreign and expensive they didn't know the name of. Marshall's car was a big, gold Bel Air. At one time his grandmother drove it to the Grand Union supermarket, to the doctor on Cottage Grove, to her friend Anna Ward's house to play Whist, and once a week to the library, where she'd pull around back and pop open the trunk, and one of the staff would take the week's return books out and cart them up the loading ramp. Because his grandmother was a Prosser, the family who founded the library in 1908, she could check out as many books as she liked. Now, she was in a convalescent home and didn't drive. In trade for the car Marshall had to do the weekly library run, and sometimes Ivy went with him to pick up the books. The librarian had them already set aside, but once in a while she'd have been too busy, and Marshall would give her a lecture about her oversight and neglect of an aged founder of that establishment, and he and Ivy scoured the shelves, yanking anything brightly covered enough to signify what Mrs. Prosser called a *tawdry romance*.

Ivy read to his grandmother at Brightview. The woman had asked her if one day she would, and then one day led to others—a summer of days in which her mother drove her, past Pettibone's Tavern and the golf course in Canton, the road finally winding through the old hardwood forest to the iron-gated entrance. Ivy sat by the window in Mrs. Prosser's room and read about young women seduced by employers, princes, spies, and gas station attendants. She read sex scenes set in ancient temples and on lake shores, described in language that made her lower her voice in embarrassment. They coupled with *frenzied writhing* and *hot, wet abandon*. The women had *downy mounds*, their breasts were *cupped* and *pressed* and *freed*. The men were *sleek and tight* and *buried themselves to the hilt*. Mrs. Prosser would lean toward Ivy to catch every word, the smell of her skin like the Tinkerbell perfume Ivy had as a child, with its pink atomizer, and its scent of lilacs. Outside, wood thrushes came one by one to the feeder. The man with braces on his legs from polio passed in the hallway. The woman in the next room called out, "Let the cat in, Louis!"

"Read that last bit again," Mrs. Prosser would say, her small eyes fiercely lit. She always fell asleep, her hand held to her chest like a pledge, the applesauce on the tray pushed aside, and Ivy kept reading, silently, the dust of the library rising up off the pages, the tree shadows *arching in wild response* on the floor.

The back seat of Marshall's grandmother's Bel Air had a hole burned into it where Laurie's cigarette blew back in without her knowing. Its fenders flaked rust and paint. It had a tape player that sometimes cut out. If they were all high, they didn't notice. They'd be sitting in Penwood, looking out at the leaves blowing over the windshield, waiting for one of Billy's friends to deliver his pot, and someone would call attention to the quiet.

"What's that?" It was usually Jonah. "That sound."

They'd all concentrate for a while on the silence. Eventually, someone mentioned the tape cutting off, and Marshall would eject and reload, eject and reload. It might take five or six times before the music came back on. That day, the tape worked right away. For some reason, they were all serious. No one smiled, or made a comment. Ivy said they looked like people about to commit a crime. The music blared, silly and unnecessary. Ivy told Marshall to turn it off.

"Where to?" Marshall asked.

"Woodfords," Ivy and Laurie said at once.

Jonah's house was a historic Federal with a barn and a slate pool and land that backed up to Talcott Mountain, that included acres of old Valley View dairy. His stepmother, Jane, as much an attraction as the house, was a woman they'd heard about from Marshall, who met her that summer when he'd gone to the house. She'd had her hair pulled up in a messy knot, and worn cut-offs and no shoes, padding around the kitchen getting them glasses of iced tea.

"Is that enough for you boys?" she'd asked. She leaned forward on the counter and her blouse opened in a V to show her breasts, and the one small, dark mole between them.

In the car now Marshall made the observation that everything Jane Woodford said seemed to carry sexual overtones.

"It's like she wants me," he said.

Billy reached over the seat and gave Marshall a good solid punch. "Have some manners," he said. "Respect your elders."

Ivy looked back at Jonah, but his face remained blank and expressionless, a look Ivy had noticed and tried unsuccessfully to read.

"I think one of you should sit back here with us," Billy said.

"Yeah, I feel segregated," Jonah said. He cupped his hands and lit a cigarette. Lately, he'd been wearing his private school shirts under a torn sweatshirt. Ivy could see the button-down collar and the shirttails. His jeans had dirt embedded in the knees from days ago, when they'd hiked up the mountain to Heublein tower, and he led them off on another trail to the ridge, to the old hang-gliding launch, an open space that gave way to the river valley below. You could hear the echo of the guns going off at the firing range, and see the toylike cars passing on Simsbury Road. Jonah had gone right up to the edge, where there was one cedar, leaning and knotted, and nothing but sky, and knelt there like a penitent in the clay-colored dirt. Laurie had gasped and told him to get back, and Billy had taken her arm and shaken his head at her, giving her a hard, serious look, so uncharacteristic she had to pay attention.

"His mother," he said, whispering.

He did a little pantomime with a cigarette in his mouth. He spread his arms out, and held then over his head like a diver. He walked his two fingers on the edge of his palm, and had them leap off. Ivy and Laurie both seemed to remember the story at the same time. Laurie's face flushed and her eyes flashed at Ivy. Billy was saying that the woman who'd leapt from the ridge years ago had been Jonah's mother. The story was as well known as the one connected to Ivy's father. The woman had gone up there alone one fall afternoon. She'd undressed and left her clothes in a neatly folded pile—a nightgown, a camel hair coat. The clothing was discovered by hikers, sodden and molding and sprouting lichen. Laurie became very quiet. Ivy tried to pretend the knowledge didn't affect her, but she wondered, the rest of the way to the top, what sent the woman to the ridge with her plan to leap off.

Everyone was too tired and winded from smoking and climbing to go up in the tower, but Ivy had wanted to do it, and she went alone. The staircase was warm, and outside the sun bounced around off the mica in the rocks. She wanted to see the valley again, and the color left in the sugar maples, and she looked out, safe behind the glass of windows labeled with their vantage point—north, south, east, and west, each revealing the same hazy view. She read about the man who'd built the place as a summer retreat in 1914, modeling it after houses in a Bavarian village, anchoring it into the bedrock so that it would withstand one-hundred-mile-an-hour winds. And Jonah came up the stairs and moved behind her as if to read about the place, too, but instead he'd put his face into her hair, and exhaled, and she could feel his chest against her back, and his heart beating through his sweatshirt. Ivy felt as lightheaded as she had standing on the ridge. Her sadness for him made her awkward and quiet. They stood with their bodies touching, and Ivy leaned into him, and he leaned into her so that she could feel him harden in his jeans. She thought: *hungry urgency, pulsing core.*

Ivy and Laurie had unspoken rules about things. When a boy chose you, he was the one you went with. There was something a little immoral about switching off. Since Laurie was prettier, Ivy was used to liking whomever she ended up with. Maybe his hair was straggly, or he had a potbelly, or a face scarred by acne. Still, there was always the possibility of some hidden attribute—an ardor to his kissing, a certain amorousness, something as simple as knowing what to do with his tongue, or where to go once he got her pants undone. Ivy had learned it was safer that they always liked her more. Liking someone too much went against everything she believed in, and the whole thing with Jonah in the tower unsettled her. Later, she wondered why she didn't take his hands and put them around her, or turn to face him, and kiss him, but maybe she'd wanted to be seduced like the women in Mrs. Prosser's romances, and for some reason that afternoon he wasn't ready to have her, or else he wasn't sure she was ready to let him. Now in the car Laurie turned and smiled at Billy and Jonah in the back seat.

"Is there room for me?" she asked.

Jonah slid over next to Billy and left a place by the passenger door. He patted the seat. "Right here on the burn hole, sweetheart," he said. Laurie tossed her hair and turned back around.

"Forget it," she said.

Ivy saw her bite her lip. Her skin was very pale, and her cheeks looked mottled from the cold. She glanced at Ivy, and her eyes still surprised her with their color—almost aqua, like the worn velvet couch in Marshall's grandmother's room at Brightview. Once, Ivy told this to Jonah, and he smiled. He said Laurie's eyes were the color of the Gulf of Mexico. Ivy said that sounded romantic, and he looked at her and shook his head.

"I didn't mean for it to," he said. His own eyes were nearly black. There was a sprinkling of acne on his nose, and a cut on his cheekbone from when he'd fallen, drunk, the night before. His lips were usually chapped, his hair dirty. Driving in a strangely quiet way that day to the Woodfords', Ivy realized that Billy was by far the better looking of the two, that she might actually end up with the boy she really wanted.

As they passed Riley's Lumber and the engine whined up the cemetery hill, it began to snow. Ivy told Marshall to pull over, and he turned into the cemetery drive and she got out and stood in the falling snow and closed her eyes. The rest of them stayed in the car. Ivy heard Laurie say, "She's been waiting for this," a soft aside. She heard Jonah make a noise, like a chuckle. Billy clambered out with a lit joint and brought it to her. They stood looking down the cemetery hill, the smoke hot and harsh in her throat, the snow landing on their shoulders like the wood shavings from Riley's.

"Sit in the back," he said softly. He looked at her from under his long, soft bangs to see if she'd heard him. Ivy looked away.

"Why should I?" she asked.

Billy shook his bangs back and put the joint to his lips. The end lit up. He exhaled and smiled. "He wants you to," he said. Ivy knew then that they'd had the discussion, that things had been decided. Billy wanted Laurie, and Jonah wanted Ivy. Billy waited for her to return to the car, to climb into the back beside Jonah, but Ivy stood in the snow falling, unable to move. This was how it always went, she thought. Nothing surprised her about Billy's request, except that this time when she got into the back seat she'd be getting what she wanted. And yet she could not. She felt something slow-building, like grief.

Ivy went back to the car and got into the front beside Laurie, who glared at her. "What are you doing?" she hissed.

Ivy said nothing, leaden now with the feeling. She heard the back car door slam, and she smelled Billy's coat, the outdoors and the snow caught in the wool. They drove on to the Woodfords', with Marshall telling them a story about the depravity of the meat packing industry, and no one saying anything in return, so that eventually he, too, stopped talking. Ivy thought maybe it was the snow, changing everything. It fell quickly, thickly, into shrubs and onto roofs and gables. They turned down Jonah's long drive, under the snow-covered arching limbs of beech trees. They went in through the sun porch, where Jane kept her *Vogue* and *Cosmopolitan* magazines, and a pair of hand-painted reading glasses. They kicked off their shoes. Jane heard them and met them in the kitchen. She had on a wool blazer and jeans and high-heeled boots.

"I was just going out," she said.

"You'd better not, Mrs. Woodford," Marshall told her.

"Is it slick?" she asked.

Marshall looked down at the toes of his white socks and snickered. In the kitchen Jonah started pulling open cabinets.

"Yeah, the roads are bad, Mrs. Woodford," Billy said. He beamed at her with glassy eyes.

"So, school's out early?" Jane said. Her boots tapped back into the kitchen.

"Jane, we're going to have a drink. Would you like one?" Jonah asked. He had glasses set out on the counter. Ivy saw Jane Woodford raise her eyebrows at him.

"Aren't you cute," she said, a little sourly.

Jonah looked up at her with that blank expression of his. "I'm having a Harvey Wallbanger," he said.

"What happened to good old hot chocolate?" she said.

But the thing they learned about Jane Woodford was that she was simply waiting for them to convince her otherwise. She was just as bored sitting around in a snowstorm as they were. She was the one who cracked open the Chardonnay, who pretended not to notice when Ivy and Laurie poured themselves a glass. They put on the news to watch the weather updates—the banner of cancellations that ran below the soap opera, the occasional interruption of a reporter waving his arm over a map of the area. The boys had gone upstairs to Jonah's wing of the house. They had the stereo on, and the chandelier shook from the bass's low end, and the little bulbs clicked off and on, so that finally Jane, annoyed, got a chair and climbed up to screw the bulbs in tighter. Ivy watched her boot heels sink into the velvet seat cushion. Jane had been in the middle of telling them a story about one of her old sorority parties. Ivy and Laurie had no intention of going to college, but they listened anyway, emptying the wine. Laurie had taken over refilling everyone's glass, and then Jane climbed down off the chair and told her where to find another bottle in the refrigerator. Laurie left for the kitchen, and Ivy and Jane sat quietly, watching the snow land on the back patio's cast-iron furniture.

"I've always liked being drunk in the middle of the afternoon," Ivy said.

Jane laughed and gave her a sideways look. She swiped her hair up off her face. "You're not like other girls, are you?" she said.

Ivy didn't know if she meant this as a compliment. They sat on the carpet in front of the couch. Laurie didn't come back, and Ivy assumed she'd gone to the bathroom, or run into someone from upstairs, maybe Billy, or Jonah, come down for a refill. She didn't imagine much more than that. Jane sighed and told Ivy her husband was probably living it up on the West Coast, where he'd gone on business. Ivy looked at her, steadily, and shrugged.

"Sometimes I wonder if he's met someone else," Jane said.

She was watching Ivy, who didn't know how to react, and looked away. Jane tapped her nails on the base of her crystal glass. Ivy glanced back at her and Jane's eyes were wet under her bangs. She leaned in. "He and I were having an affair," she whispered, her mouth very soft and pillowy, close to Ivy's face. "Before his wife left." Ivy smelled Jane's perfume on the collar of her blouse, the wine on her breath. Jane shook back her soft hair and sipped from her glass. Ivy paled a little, picturing Jonah's mother learning the news, making her desperate plans. Jane squinted at her.

"He told you she jumped from the ridge, didn't he?"

Ivy opened her mouth to respond, and then she understood that Billy had lied to them, that Jonah had told him to. Jane made a disgusted face.

"That woman is alive and well in Suffield with a whole new family. I think he almost believes his own little story."

And it must have been the way Ivy looked at her, differently, assessing, imagining her on the edge of a motel bed with a phone pressed to her ear, fanning red fingernails. Jane shifted around so that she faced Ivy, and pressed her forehead against Ivy's. "Don't blame me," she said. "I'm so tired of being blamed."

Ivy thought she should pull away from her, but she did not.

Their foreheads settled hard and bony against each other. Maybe this was what best friends in sororities did together, Ivy thought. Divulged secrets, shared tremendous burdens. She could feel Jane's breath and her lips on her cheek. *In 1803, English pharmacist Luke Howard created the Latin name for these billowy clouds that can build to heights of 39,000 feet* . . . "Cumulus."

And then Jonah came to the doorway. He gave them his bland look, one that Ivy now understood meant they should never feel sorry for him. Jane pulled back and ran her hands through her hair. She gave a little false laugh.

"Are you ready?" he asked Ivy.

Ivy and Jane stared at him.

"What's going on?" Jane said.

Jonah had turned away from her and now he glanced back. "We're taking the snowmobiles out," he said.

Ivy stood and joined him in the doorway. Billy and Laurie came down the stairs—Billy's fingers threaded through one of her belt hoops, Laurie's shirt misbuttoned. Marshall was in the kitchen, filling containers with peppermint schnapps and Yukon Jack—a tarnished silver flask etched with a monogram, another that resembled a leather pouch with a strap, and an old canteen. There was a thermos, and a plastic Rubbermaid quart container that Jonah decided was too big.

"For who?" Marshall said, waggling his eyebrows.

Billy had Laurie up against the pantry doors, his hands along her waist, under her shirt where you could see her skin exposed, as pale as that on her face. They kissed, their mouths hidden by Laurie's hair. Jane joined Marshall at the counter and nudged him, playfully, with her elbow.

"I'm coming, too," she said, ready for an adventure.

Ivy saw Marshall and Billy exchange looks. Jane handed out coats from the depths of a walk-in closet under the stairs. Down parkas with tags from Sundown and Sugarbush and Stowe, the pockets filled with old lozenges and gum wrappers, a receipt from a convenience store, a plastic-wrapped tampon, matchbooks and a folded five-dollar bill—things they laid on the counter before they left, like relics. Everyone trudged out the sunroom and up the path to the barn. In the summer this was gravel, lined with lilies. The pool lay to the left, covered with vinyl and the snow that continued to fall, heavy and wet, icing up the hems of their jeans. All around, everything was new and white and different. Ivy didn't feel the cold. Jonah had come up to her and put a ski cap on her head, tugging it down to cover her ears. He did it the way you might dress a child, his face serious and intent. Ivy wondered if he thought he had to pretend he cared for her to have her, if maybe that was what she'd wanted all along, and he sensed it. The wool cap, the snowfall, muffled the world. Inside the barn it smelled like something combustible—gasoline and hay—and arrayed on a wall of shelves was an assortment of yard games—rolled badminton nets and baskets of shuttlecocks, croquet mallets, and wickets. There were rakes and shovels and bags of lime and ornamental pine bark. Jonah's car sat in the middle of it all—not a sports car but an old Mercedes with a sky-blue paint job.

"Oh, I miss those days," Billy said, placing his gloved hands on the hood, gently, reverently. He and Jonah stood side by side by the front bumper, and Ivy heard Billy say to him, "Maggie Simons, Amie Blackwell, Deirdre Compton," and Jonah say back, "Check, Check, Check-plus."

The snowmobiles were lined up along one wall, and Jane leaned against the car, giving them a dubious look. She wore a hat with a pompom. Her face looked tired, and older. As the boys filled the snowmobile's tanks, she stood over them, asking them if they knew what they were doing.

"How much experience do you have?" she wanted to know.

"Oh, we're experienced," Marshall said. "Trust me, Mrs. Woodford."

Billy handed her the silver flask. "You're the keeper of the liquor," he said.

Jane unscrewed the top and took a drink. "Jesus, Mary, and Joseph," she said under her breath.

The snowmobiles started right up. Jonah took hold of Ivy's jacket sleeve, ensuring that she rode with him. Jane rode with Marshall, who had the least experience. Ivy imagined he'd never driven a snowmobile before. That, along with the distraction of Jane's body against his, the presence of her thighs and arms, her peppermint breath in his ear, may have complicated everything even more. Billy and Laurie led the way down the drive, out to the unplowed road, and they wound along to the Heublein tower entrance and started up the trail. Ivy knew that Billy and Jonah had probably ridden these trails for years, but they were treacherous ones in the fading light and the falling snow. The snowmobiles' headlights cut long swaths, but often there were unexpected dips that the beams couldn't pick up, that lifted her off the seat and flung her about. She imagined that the Chardonnay and the shots of schnapps weren't enough to fortify Jane against her apprehension. She could hear her shrieks through the whine of the engines, and when they stopped to have a drink Jane got off and trudged over to Jonah.

"I think it's time we head back," she said. They were under a canopy of pine, and it was warmer without the rush of wind. Jane's breath came out in a white plume. Her nose was red. Probably, this was the voice she used the times she'd tried to be a mother to him. Jonah looked up at her, askance. He wore an absurd hat with flaps over his ears.

"What's that?" he said, lifting one of the flaps.

Billy had lit a joint, and held it cupped in his palm. "It's not much farther," he said. "You'll make it."

I saw then that they were heading for the ridge. Jonah lifted a leg over and swiveled around to face Ivy. He took off his gloves and found the leather flask, tipped it back, and took a drink. His mouth was red, and wet. Jane's eyes pleaded with Ivy to relent. Jonah put his cold fingers on Ivy's chin and turned her face so she'd look at him.

"You're okay, right?" he said.

Jonah Woodford will be the first of a long line of boys she will come to recognize, steering around them carefully, leery of being drawn in. They are unflinching, unforgiving. They reveal nothing. Their souls have been rent and cauterized. That evening the snow fell in the snowmobile headlights and Jonah waited for something from her—a smile, a weakening. Jane tromped over to Billy and Laurie and began imploring them to turn around. Ivy heard her voice, higher-pitched and disbelieving. She heard her change tactics, promise a warm fire, and more liquor. "Anything," she said finally. "Just get me off this mountain." Jonah kept his face close to Ivy's. As easy as it would have been to kiss his cold, wet mouth, and ask him to turn around, she didn't.

Ivy and Jonah led the rest of the way to the ridge. She didn't look to see who followed them. She half-expected to fly off the edge of the mountain, and she waited for the moment, with dread, and exhilaration, with a surrender she has never felt since. But Jonah knew when to slow and inch closer and stop. The snowmobile headlight marked the black sky. Someone joined them and Ivy turned to see Billy and Laurie. The engines cut off, and she heard Laurie crying, and Billy laughing at her.

"I hate you," Laurie said.

Ivy buried her face against Jonah's parka and heard him clear his throat, a boyish, nervous sound. They passed the flask around, and waited for Marshall and Jane. They could hear the snowmobile engine in the distance. Jonah had a cigarette. As he smoked he told them about King Philip's War, and the cave that existed below the ridge. Once, King Philip sat in his cave overlooking this valley and watched the warring tribes skirmish. The bodies fell and bled into the loamy soil.

"He sat in it and watched his warriors burn the town to the ground," he said. He threw his cigarette down into the snow, and all they could hear was the wind.

"This is where that woman jumped from," Ivy said. She didn't know what made her say it. Laurie's eyes widened. Ivy saw Billy glance down at his boots. Jonah shifted a little on the seat. He looked back at Ivy. "Yeah, you're right," he said. She thought she saw a trace of a smile.

They sat listening for Marshall and Jane a while longer. Billy said maybe they'd turned back. They never heard anything more, and so they assumed they'd turned around, that Marshall could follow the trail down. They never went back the way they came, or tried to look for them. After the ridge they took another route through the woods and stopped at a wooden building that looked at night like another small barn, except that inside were bunks with a few rolled-up sleeping bags, and a kerosene lantern and a fireplace. Billy and Jonah lit the lantern and made a fire, and Ivy could see a stack of board games—Parcheesi and Risk, their boxes mottled with mildew, and a yellowed map of the valley tacked to the wall. The two boys sat at an old Formica-covered table with metal legs, and Ivy and Laurie sat on the floor in front of the fire on one of the sleeping bags. It smelled of dust and damp, and faintly, of a man's cologne. Laurie's eyes were red from crying, and when she smoked a cigarette her hand shook. She kept giving Ivy looks, and seemed not frightened but confused. They were mute from the cold and the liquor. Ivy felt the heat of the flames on her face and kept imagining herself plummeting from the ridge, even though the worst of what might have happened to them was over by then, and all that was left was what they'd planned from the beginning, having sex in this place where there were probably condoms in one of the kitchen drawers, and more liquor stashed up above the sink. In the summer they left the windows open and the night noises and the mosquitoes came in, and the girls left with dime-sized bites, and knotted hair smelling of camphor. It wasn't any use trying to make these boys love them. They knew that all along. But maybe Laurie had hoped it, and maybe even Ivy had, for a moment, longed to be viewed as someone other than what she'd amounted to at the time.

The boys drank and sat talking quietly together, pretending to ignore them. The lantern made hollows in the planes of their faces. Ivy and Laurie listened in and learned that this was an old hunting lodge they'd come to with their fathers. They overheard their stories of deer kills, and spilled blood, and skinnings, and how Jonah threw up in the snow, and his father had called him a pussy, and Jonah had hit him.

"Once, right in the face," he said. "My glove was all iced up, and it cut him under the eye."

"How'd it feel?" Billy asked.

"It felt good," Jonah said. "Really good."

His voice held a certain amount of amazed tightness, as if he hadn't ever spoken about the incident before. The fire warmed the place up, and Ivy could almost imagine she was where she wanted to be. Eventually the boys put out the lantern and unrolled sleeping bags onto the bunks on either side of the room. Ivy could hear the creaking of the wood boards as they stretched out. She and Laurie waited, and then Billy called Laurie over, plaintively. "It's cold over here, sweetheart," he said. And she got up gratefully and Ivy heard her boots clomping across the floor into the dark part of the room. She imagined, foolishly, Jane settled into her comfortable bed, the old house's furnace chugging on, her feet warming up under the covers. That Marshall had found a place on the couch in the family room, or Jane had given him a bed in the guest room, or that miraculously, out of gratitude and a slight drunkenness, something had actually happened between them, and Marshall would have a story to confess to Ivy and Laurie sitting on the low wall of the smoking pavilion at school, his feet shuffling the crushed butts, his breath a cloud fogging his glasses.

Ivy stretched out in front of the fire and put her head on her folded arms. The snow blew in spurts against the windows. It piled in drifts around doors and covered porch steps. The police drove cruisers with chains on the tires through the unplowed neighborhoods—up Foothills Way and down Butternut Drive, monitoring everyone's safety. Ivy imagined herself in her own bed in her room, and her parents' closed door across the hall, and the clank of the cruisers' chains past the house. In Brightview, Marshall's grandmother might feel the presence of the snow against her room's plate glass window. The heat would be on. She'd wear a quilted robe and the mohair afghan pulled up around her. Ivy imagined herself on her aqua-colored couch, reading: *He mastered her mouth and her body until she was weeping with it*. Mrs. Prosser's eyelids fluttered, pale and veined.

In the dark lodge Ivy listened to Billy's heavy breaths, the rustling of clothes, Laurie's soft assents. Jonah lay alone in his bunk. He didn't need warmth, or sex, or anyone's love. His and Ivy's silences complemented each other, their bodies separated and resigned to other places—his back at the ridge, the snow and the height dizzying. And hers held fast to the silty bottom of the river where the woman takes a final breath of brackish water, where the ice moves in, and then the thaw, until it is a spring day above, the currents swift and tugging her arms, the boats cutting the surface, churning the water on their way to Duck Island for picnic lunches. Buttercups bloom on the banks. The buoys bob and drag. Hornets nest in the rotting pilings. The shad and trout and river herring nibble her limbs, her face, take small stinging bites, their tails thrashing and quick. The seaweed tangles in her hair.

Jonah rose from his bunk. Ivy heard his footsteps approach and then he was beside her on the floor. He lay back and stared up at the ceiling. They listened together to Billy's last moan, and the ensuing quiet. Their arms touched, and nothing else. Ivy and Laurie will have this one night with these two boys, and then the boys will be done with them. The next day they will learn of the accident, and of Marshall carrying Jane all night down the mountain to stumble onto freshly plowed Simsbury Road and the morning traffic. Marshall will survive to show them his foot without the toes lost to frostbite. Jane's face, blue-tinged, eyes open and accusing, her pretty hair frozen with blood and snow, will haunt him for years. Ivy and Laurie will share a guilty feel-ing, a smothering sense of loss before they part ways and there are other boys. That night in the lodge Ivy turned on her side and looked at Jonah, his profile calm and emotionless, waiting for her to close the space between them, to do what he had heard she did best. But she is a smart girl who will not be used. *The force of the heart's contraction arises from what muscular tissue?* she asked him. Below the ridge houses sat tucked into the mountain, the people in them shadows passing lit windows with cups of tea. Only Ivy sees the woman's body he sends tumbling, white and languid past the ghost of old King Philip.

Housewifery

In our neighborhood there is a walking path. We consider ourselves lucky to have such a thing, neatly paved with black tar like
our driveways, cutting between Capes and Colonials and imitation Saltboxes, through our own safe, scenic woods, circling
the elementary school's playing field, connecting one street with
another. It is summer when we discover that someone has veered
off the path and made one of their own leading up a wooded
hill through wild blackberry and fern. Our children clamor for
the adventure of the new path. We suspect teenagers, ferreting
out their secret places to congregate, to do what we remember
doing when we were their age, and we hesitate. We would feel
obligated to put a stop to what we find, and no one wants to be,
as Jane Filley says, "Old Mrs. Brunner with her mothball breath
and cranky threats," who used to chase her and her friends out
of their neighborhood woods.

Maura Stahl is the first to try the path. Her children are three
and five—Sylvia and Max—and she tells them to leave their bikes
where the path diverges, which happens to be the Currys' backyard, close to the slate patio and the carefully arranged cast-iron
furniture. Maura takes the children's hands firmly in hers, even
though Max protests that he can walk himself. It is midday. The
heat dissolves in the cool woods. Maura allows Max to walk
ahead, because as soon as they maneuver past the blackberry's

thorns, they discover well-trodden dirt that leads up the hillside, mossy and speckled with sunlight. This dirt path curves through saplings and shade fragrant with pine. There are large rocks, boulders that appear to have tumbled down off a mountain that no longer exists, or emerged from the leaf-strewn floor of the woods like something from the core of the earth, and she lets the children scramble on their surfaces, shows Max how with a small stone he can etch his name and his sister's name boldly on the flat face. They walk for ten minutes, "no more than that," she tells us. And just when she thinks she will turn around, she sees sunlight up ahead and steps into a clearing—a flat sunny place filled with meadow grass and a pond. We are disbelieving, of course.

"What sort of *pond*?" Jane Filley asks.

Maura smiles. "Fresh water," she tells us. "It's more like a swimming hole, fed by this beautiful running brook."

We are surrounded by Algonquian place names, those the early settlers of the 1670s must have once understood—*Mashamoquet, Susquetonscut, Quinnatisset*; big fish place, place of red ledges, little long river. These now signify parks and country clubs and shopping plazas. The idea of an actual brook, and a pond, of all things, shouldn't be too hard for us to accept. And still we cannot believe it until someone catches Maura heading up the new path with folding beach chairs and a canvas tote stuffed with towels.

"Do you think she is letting them *swim*?" we ask each other. "Aren't there leeches? Snakes? Actual fish?"

Soon others go and are spotted returning, the children's faces suntanned and serene.

"It's so peaceful," they proclaim. "The birds flit around. The kids splash in the brook and catch frogs. They swim in the shallows."

Some of the mothers swim themselves—the water ice-cold and clear. "You can see the sandy bottom. The little fish."

"We bring lunch," they tell us. "We talk."

They explore the woods and find the stone remains of a homesite, the rocks toppled into piles along the foundation, sprung from their places by frost and spring thaw, by passing fox and deer and clumsy hunters. Once this area was an open field, long before hickory and oak grew to fill it in. A family plowed and planted hills of rocky soil where our houses sit. The settlers had their own names for places: Mount Misery, Bare Hill, Hell Hollow. Someone mentions researching the site, but this idea is quickly discarded. We've heard about family gravesites and ghost legends from teenagers who seek them out on Halloween: the grave of the two-year-old girl who died of diphtheria, whose grief-stricken mother saved the apple she'd eaten that held her little tooth prints, the woods haunted by screams of a Native American woman murdered by British soldiers. We don't want to know too much.

Now at all times of day women tramp up and down the wooded path. Those with children who nap, those who've scheduled dentist appointments and music lessons, drag back early, the children angry and crying. We don't worry about the Currys seeing women and children passing through their backyard, treading a path through their grass. The Currys' son, Michael, is college-aged, off somewhere in Europe, someone's heard. Both Walt and Kate Curry work in Hartford—Walt as an engineer, Kate as an attorney. If she were home, she'd certainly notice us as she rinsed her dishes at the kitchen sink. Their house is a Colonial, one of the first built in the neighborhood. There are French doors leading out to the patio, and Jane Filley swears one day that she saw Kate standing there wearing an apron, yellow plastic gloves, and smoking a cigarette. The door was cracked, and the smoke snaked out, a thin white cloud.

"I could smell it," Jane says. "She looked like my mother used to, standing there."

We all know what she means—our mothers with their hairspray and L'Air du Temps, with their bold print dresses, everyone back then reaching into coat pockets and purses for their cigarettes the moment they came out of church—the church the only place they couldn't smoke. We don't know why Kate Curry is home during the day. We expect she will emerge now to order us off her property, and we consider the necessity of making another path, but only briefly. When Kate does make herself known, it isn't in the way we expect. It is a Wednesday afternoon. Most of us have dinner planned—meat defrosting, vegetables already cut and placed in Tupperware, and so we linger. The children make a fort, towels draped over sticks. They build it on the sandy bank and play house, pretending to cook over a fire for their own imaginary families. Maura has remembered the bug spray, so we stay, lounging by the pond, watching the water striders skate across the surface where it is still and deep.

Heading back we always feel what we've come to call the end-of-the-day sadness. A weightiness that arrives with summer. We are reminded of summers of our youth—the lawn cool in the mornings, the sun just coming up, and a breeze moving the drapes of our bedrooms. Our fathers have gotten up and gone to work. Our mothers are talking to their mothers on the phone, or watering zinnias, or absently stirring their coffee, the clink of the spoon inside their cups a sound we now make ourselves. The whole day stretches before us, a luxury we feel each time we tread the path up to the pond and that is depleted as the day draws to an end. As children we thought summer was interminable, but as adults we know otherwise. It is in this mood that we descend and emerge from the woods toting our bags and towels and assorted toys, the children singing something from television. We step onto freshly mown grass and meet Kate Curry.

She wears a pair of shorts and a white sleeveless blouse. Her hair is pulled back in a neat ponytail. Around her eyes are the fine lines we notice on everyone but ourselves. She waves and invites us all inside. "For a snack," she says. And then she squats down in front of our children the way they tell you to do when you speak to them, and says, "You'd like a snack, wouldn't you? A popsicle? An ice cream cup?"

We thank her but beg off. "So close to suppertime," we say.

But she knows the children will plead and make it impossible to drag them off. It isn't that we don't want to go into her house, but that we have our minds set on getting home, on taking our burden of unspoken sadness back to our own crumb-littered counters and sagging couch cushions, to the book we left open on our nightstands. But the children and Kate win out, and we all file through the French doors into her spotless kitchen. The children are shown the den and the television where they can sit with their ice cream. Kelsey Simons asks for a place to change the baby, and Kate shows her the bathroom, and then the place to put the sodden diaper. All of us seem to fill up Kate's house. We sprawl at the kitchen table, and she offers us a drink—"Gin? Vodka?"—and we laugh, even though we sense it will offset the end-of-the-day feeling. And then Maura pipes up, her broad face rosy from the sun. "I'll take whatever you've got."

Now we always end the day at Kate's. We tromp down and Kate is waiting, and the children get their Popsicles or pretzel sticks, and we get our sloe gin fizzes, or tequila sunrises, or Tom Collinses. Sometimes we sit in the yard on her rarely used cast-iron furniture or in our folding chairs, the aluminum legs still covered with brook sand. Kate serves us all from a tray. She asks us about the pond, our day, where we'll vacation, an inevitable breach in our routine. Everyone has someplace to go each summer—to the mountains in New Hampshire, to Nantucket, or to the beach house at Point O'Woods. We don't all go at once, but the missing woman and children are acknowledged like place cards at a table. Kate remembers where everyone is going, and when.

"Jane's off to Franconia," she says. She gives the children calamine lotion for their bites. She sprays on Bactine and blows on their small injured knees. She is our mother, our friend, our benefactress. She advises us what to wear to our husbands' company functions, to the club for lunch with our husbands' mothers. With Kate we wear our five-year-old bathing suits, the elastic sprung, T-shirts stained with jelly, spit-up, dirty handprints. She knows the women we become when we put on our black sheath dresses, our grandmother's pearls. No one asks Kate why she's left her job. We don't inquire about her son, Michael, off to Europe. We imagine him trekking the Alps with a backpack, studying the flora. We picture him a biologist, an entomologist, someone who will one day work in a university. There are photos of him as a child wearing glasses, a sandy-haired boy with bony arms and legs. From these images we can create any future we like. His absence is something we accept, like our husbands'. Kate's grown son has simply been swallowed up by the same world where they reside—a childless place, filled with *work, lunch, meetings.*

Eventually, women from surrounding neighborhoods with ties to our walking path discover the pond, stake out their places with bedspreads and towels. They are from Pudding Hill, Whittle Lane, Bennett's Hollow, names stolen by developers from early town founders. They bring floats for the children. They bring a two-man raft with paddles. They plant umbrellas and dole out cups of lemonade from large thermoses. On any given day you will find them at Kate's—women we do not even know sitting in their folding chairs on Kate's soft grass, or changing babies, their children running up and down Kate's driveway, drawing on the tarred surface with colored chalk. She will always make introductions. She keeps diapers and snacks for the little ones. On days when thunderheads threaten lightening and rain we are always at a loss, planning trips to the movies, to the bowling alley or the Children's Museum. But no one wonders about Kate. Jane thinks she is having a fine day free of us and our boisterous children with their demands and quarrels and uncontested needs. We never think to invite her along.

It is late August, when the sunlight through the trees is different, the pond's water altered to a deeper color, that we discover Kate's secret. She is ready to share it with us, her *little hobby,* and while the children play in the den she leads a group of us with our drinks down the basement steps. We imagine painted bookshelves or restored antique chairs. We picture, in the recesses of the basement, a sewing machine and the old-timey patterns we sewed in home economics, or yards of brocade upholstery. We clutch the wooden rail and step carefully. It is dim and smells, much as our basements do, of mildew, damp, and laundry soap. Jane Filley says, "Where's the light?" and stumbles around looking for the string pull for an overhead bulb, but Kate says to wait, and she flips a switch somewhere ahead of us in the darkness, and the room illuminates, a cavernous space decorated, inexplicably, for Christmas.

She has tacked up swags of fake greens filled with tiny white lights along the ceiling, threaded among the exposed pipes. There are imitation Fraser firs covered with balls and ribbons and tinsel, and those mechanical dolls dressed in Victorian garb, their mouths opening and closing to music we cannot hear. There are fake deer that dip their heads to eat and raise them to listen for predators, a miniature town set up on a large platform covered with fluffy snow-batting—churches and stores and houses, a mirror pond with ice skaters, a train doing its mechanical whir around the perimeter. There are ornaments that later Jane surmises must be the result of years of collecting—Nutcrackers, angels with trumpets, glass fruit covered with glitter. We ooh and aah, make the expected noises. We do not understand. Is it for the children? What is it?

Maura widens her eyes and is the first to make an excuse to leave. She has the meatloaf still, she explains. She is up the stairs before anyone can stop her. Jane goes on nonstop about Christmas being her favorite holiday, and how there was one house in her neighborhood that really did it up big, and we knew her chattering was done as a kindness to fill the silence. The rest of us make a show of walking about and fingering ornaments, commenting on their uniqueness. One of us trips over an extension cord and a drink spills its bright tropical colors onto the pristine village snow. We all watch Kate's face lose its softness, stiffen with apprehension.

"Oh, don't worry about it," she tells us. She laughs and waves her hand, but no one is convinced.

We end up standing in a small group by the stairs. "This is lovely," we say. "This is so creative."

"It isn't *normal* to have Christmas in your basement," Maura says later. We surmise that Kate has had to find a way to channel litigious energy. We notice her husband's car easing into the driveway late at night and imagine her waiting all evening for him to return, gluing plastic carolers outside a miniature snow-covered house. Those of us with our own secrets silently excuse Kate's hobby, feel almost traitorous about our reactions when she shared it with us. Still, the basement Christmas throws everything into strange relief. Nothing is as it once seemed. Sylvia Stahl's poison ivy now merits a trip to the pediatrician. Three-year-old Michael Rassmussen goes missing while we luxuriate on the pond's banks, talking about our old boyfriends. We search for a frantic ten minutes until he is found farther down the brook, pretending to catch fish with a stick and a piece of string. We are tired at the end of the day, more tired than we have ever been before. The housework isn't done; the laundry piles up. Dark mold grows in the cracks of the shower stall. All we need are our bathing suits, washed out each night in the sink. It is an addiction, the haze, the dappled leaf shadow, the sound of running water. We hope for Indian summer.

And then August has ended, the start of school looms, and we climb the path with heavy dread. "The leaves can't be changing?" someone muses. The dragonflies are gone. The field is filled with late-summer flowers: bluestem, lobelia, purple coneflower. The children know. They putter in the sand. They ask for sweaters. They huddle at our feet and listen to us talking about school shopping and sales and volunteer opportunities. We are sitting in our circle when Maura's husband appears, his leather soles flattening the drying grass, his dress shirt white like a signal flag. Heads pivot and pivot back, our faces without affect, poised for what might happen next. We suspect heart attack, stroke, car accident. And then as the moment expands—job termination, bankruptcy, foreclosure. All of it a loss we steel ourselves against, none of it making much sense here at the pond, with the brook's gurgling, and the wind in the leaves.

Sylvia jumps up. "It's Daddy!" she cries.

We realize it is Friday, the start of the Labor Day weekend, the offices closing early. We understand we should all be home planning our last cookout. Maura's husband approaches, scanning the area. Maura rises from her chair to meet him, and we hear his voice, the tone of it troubling. "*This* is where you've been bringing the children?"

We suddenly see the trampled-down grass, the pond's dull reflection, the scattered toys and paper cups. We instinctively cover our stretched-out suits and our bug-bitten legs, smooth down our unruly hair with its neglected roots. How can it be almost fall? The cicadas wind up and die down, the silence something no one can bear. We long for their whir, the treachery of the sound. Maura's husband steps up to the pond and looks down into it. His reflection wavers on the surface.

"You know there might be fertilizer runoff here," he says. "Contaminants." He thinks he will collect a sample and send it to the EPA for analysis.

On the way down, the end-of-the-day feeling overpowers us. Kate's house is quiet and she is nowhere. The children tap on the French doors until we order them away. We don't know what to make of any of this, or what we have become, or what the use of it all was.

The summer fades. Jane Filley gets a part-time job while her children are in school. She is a clerk in the town hall, and wears sweater sets and talks about the townspeople who come in with requests for permits and variances. Maura is pulled over while driving Max to soccer practice. "One glass of wine," she insists. "That was all I had." One or two of us join the local theater group, or volunteer for the Prison Store where items hand-carved by prisoners are sold: towel racks, finials, bedposts. We become homeroom moms and bake for school fund-raisers. We plan meals with care, fold our husband's undershirts and place them in the drawer the way he likes. When Kate and Walt Curry divorce we learn that Kate's son was not in Europe after all, examining insects for an academic thesis. He died the December before of an undisclosed illness. We tell each other we couldn't have known. We agree there was nothing we could have done, but each of us holds the flutter of doubt, the dark brushing of its wings.

Early winter, we see the Realtor's sign go up in front of the Currys' house, and we watch the house being emptied out. We see the dismantling of the basement through our living room windows—the evergreen swags, shards of colored glass, metallic bows, white false snow all set out in a trash can by the curb. The early settlers buried their children in family cemeteries. But the two-year-old girl who has become part of local legend had a lone grave, separate from her siblings, placed on a rise of land visible from the house's second-story window. Here her mother would have paused, her arms heavy with laundry or firewood, with another child on her hip, and then moved on to the baking of bread, to the planting of her garden, to the demands of the house that bring forgetfulness. Someone sees Kate Curry at Shaw's Supermarket, her hair dyed a new color. She's gotten an offer with a firm in New York City, or Boston. She is spending the winter at a friend's villa in Tortola. Some of us still go alone up the secret path through the woods. We see the trees fan out like a blaze, the pond coated with ice. We watch the fog settle among the bare, black branches, and the snow fall, its obscuring blanket. We long for the sun in our hair, the children's voices, high and happy. Each passing day, filled with the work of our lives, is its own solace.

IN THE PRAIRIE SCHOONER
BOOK PRIZE IN FICTION SERIES

Last Call: Stories
By K. L. Cook

Carrying the Torch: Stories
By Brock Clarke

Nocturnal America
By John Keeble

The Alice Stories
By Jesse Lee Kercheval

*Our Lady of the Artichokes and
Other Portuguese-American Stories*
By Katherine Vaz

Call Me Ahab: A Short Story Collection
By Anne Finger

Bliss and Other Short Stories
By Ted Gilley

Destroy All Monsters, and Other Stories
By Greg Hrbek

Little Sinners, and Other Stories
By Karen Brown

To order or obtain more
information on these or other
University of Nebraska Press titles,
visit www.nebraskapress.unl.edu.